W9-BSW-710

A Many Feathered Thing is published by Capstone Editions, an imprint of Capstone
1710 Roe Crest Drive
North Mankato, Minnesota 56003
www.capstonepub.com

Library of Congress Cataloging-in-Publication Data is available on the Library of Congress website.

ISBN: 978-1-68446-071-7 (hardcover)
ISBN: 978-1-68446-072-4 (eBook PDF)

Summary: Eleven-year-old Clara is known as the "girl who draws," but she's not tortured enough to become a real artist. Her only suffering, besides embarrassment over her real name, is a crippling inability to speak in public. When Clara and her oldest friend, Orion, break their neighbor's glass gazing ball, Clara decides that in order to suffer like a true artist, she will do every hard thing in her path . . . starting with knocking on scary old Mr. Vogelman's door. That's when she meets "Birdman." That's when she sees his swirling painting. And that's when everything changes.

Image Credits:
Cover and interior art by Rosanna Tasker
Author photo by Chelsea Starner

Designed by Tracy McCabe

Printed and bound in China. 2494

FOR ANNABEL,

WHO FEATHERS THE LIGHT TOO

CAPSTONE EDITIONS
a capstone imprint

A Many Feathered Thing

After the funeral, Orion asked me what I would have said if I had been up there in front of all those people.

"If you could choke out the words, Clara," he said.

I swatted his arm. He knew my tongue swelled like a bloated fish at the thought of speaking in front of people. But he also knew it used to be worse.

Orion's question got me thinking, though. What would I have said about Birdman? How could I have found the words for everything he'd taught me? It wasn't until later, when the finches left the flowering plum to fly up and up, that I knew the answer.

I would have talked about the wings. His and mine and everybody's.

But to understand any of that, we have to go back. Back before the portrait arrived on my doorstep. Back before everything changed.

Fall. One month into sixth grade. The gray days of Oregon rain hadn't yet begun.

The glass ball had always been there, perched on a stone pedestal at the dead end of Rock Street. It marked the start of Mr. Vogelman's driveway. None of us kids ventured past the pedestal—not under any circumstances. No one even trick-or-treated at his big, run-down house. Mr. Vogelman would probably call the cops. Rumor was he collected children's teeth . . . where he got them or what he kept them for, no one knew.

But that glass ball called to me. It had for years. It was as large as a bowling ball and darkened by bird poop and wet leaves. I always wondered what I would see if I scraped away the gunk. Did it swirl with mystery, like a crystal ball? Or was it empty on the inside?

That day, the day everything started, Orion was demonstrating his latest knot as we walked our afternoon circuit of Rock Street. Orion loved to build and make things and was always learning new skills. Lately, it was knots. Sometimes we played a game where he tied knots, and I had to untie them. But today he was showing off.

"It's called a honda knot. First I tie an overhand knot, like this."

"Mm-hmm." I tried to sound interested, but really I was thinking about the painting course that started next week at the local arts association. Over the summer, Mom and Dad had promised to sign me up. I was finally going to learn to paint with real acrylic paint. On real canvas.

I'd wanted to become an artist ever since I'd learned how to hold a crayon. Back when speaking was impossible, even with therapy, drawing had been my way of telling the world what I felt. Now I had words, but they were never as expressive as lines and shadows and color. I couldn't control words the way I could a pencil.

"Then I pass the end through," Orion was saying, "and tighten. Cool, huh?"

We had reached the dead end and the entrance to Mr. Vogelman's long, overgrown driveway, which we passed every day. The glass ball stood alone there atop its stone pedestal.

I looked at Orion's knot. "Hey, it's a lasso!"

"What did ya think I was tying? Watch this."

Orion lengthened the loop until it was as large as a Hula-Hoop. Then he twirled it over his head. At first it threatened to drop down on him like some heavy jungle snake, but as he got going, it spun like a real cowboy's lasso.

Orion grinned like a fool. Even though no one else was

watching, I felt embarrassed for my friend. Pale and freckled, with skinny legs and cotton shorts, Orion made an idiotic cowboy. Not that I could criticize looks—my huge glasses and curtains of hair weren't exactly the epitome of cool.

"I've been practicing," he drawled. "Watch."

Orion's tongue poked out of the side of his mouth as the lasso whirled, and he set his sights on the pedestal. When he let go, the rope flew with all the grace of an airborne snake. Miraculously, he lassoed the ball.

"Yee-haw!" I said.

Orion leaned back to tighten the loop, but the rope wouldn't slide through the knot.

"Pull harder," I said.

"It's supposed to tighten," he argued.

"You're not pulling hard enough," I told him. I yanked on the rope, and the lasso tightened. "See?" I said. "Show it who's boss."

I didn't feel bad bossing him around. That was just our relationship. Orion and I had been friends since our mothers put us in a crib together as infants and I clobbered him. I had been a fat baby. Orion had always been small and sickly. He was named after the constellation of a mighty hunter, but that's a lot to live up to. Maybe that's why I felt the need to help and protect him.

Orion grinned and kept pulling, leaning back to use his full body weight.

"Be careful," I warned.

Too late.

The rope tightened between the ball and the pedestal, then slid right through. Orion fell on his butt. As I watched in horror, the glass ball teetered one way, tipped the other way, and fell to the packed gravel with a sickening *craaack*.

I froze, breath caught in my chest. But the ball didn't stop. It bowled over a slick of leaves, dove off the curb, and rolled to rest on the drainage grate.

There was a moment of silence. Then Orion said, "That was not supposed to happen."

All at once, I realized we were in trouble. There would be lectures, grounding, months of Saturday chores from our parents. And what would Mr. Vogelman do? I didn't have any teeth to spare.

I helped Orion to his feet, and we crept toward the ball's final resting place. I crossed my fingers. *Please, let it be whole. Please, let it be whole.*

We crouched before it.

"Maybe it's not broken," I said hopefully. The side I could see had no cracks or chinks, only a nub of metal sticking out one end where it had been attached to the pedestal.

Orion shook his head. "You heard the crack."

I reached out to touch the ball. It felt cold and slippery under my hands. Carefully I rolled it over. Sure enough, a bolt-of-lightning crack streaked from top to bottom.

Suddenly I got all squeamish. I couldn't look into the crack. I'd always imagined something magical inside—like me. But what if I was fooling myself? What if it cracked open and revealed an ordinary nothing?

Orion got up to inspect the pedestal where a twin metal nub protruded.

"No wonder the rope went through. It's rusty." He picked off some orange flakes. "That's where it attached, but I don't think we can fix it."

That sealed the deal for me. "Let's get out of here."

"We can't just leave."

"OK, we'll set the ball back on the pedestal and *then* leave."

"I don't know . . ."

"It was bound to fall off sooner or later," I argued. "You said yourself it's rusted through. Besides, how would Mr. Vogelman know it was us?" I was on a roll of good reasoning. "There are tons of suspects. Austin and Tyler are always rowdy. And McKenna rides her tricycle like a maniac."

"Clara."

"What?" I snapped. I knew what was coming. Orion

could be annoyingly honest. If a sign said *Keep Off the Grass,* Orion wouldn't set a toe into it. Personally, I wanted to know there was a good reason not to.

"We broke something that isn't ours."

"Technically, *you* broke it," I reminded him.

Orion nodded, looking serious. "You're right. I have to confess. I have to take the ball to Mr. Vogelman's door." He shivered as he said it.

I stopped arguing. As much as I gave Orion a hard time, I knew where his relentless honesty came from. His biological father lived in another state and was always making plans with him, then canceling at the last minute. Orion tried to hide his disappointment, but I saw it. And I knew he never wanted to let someone down like that, so he always kept his word.

I sighed. I couldn't run out on him now.

"Fine, we'll do it together."

Orion shot me a grateful glance, and together we hoisted the ball. It was heavier than expected, and we had to shuffle sideways up the long gravel drive. I felt a chill as soon as we passed from sunlight to shadow. Orion's arms broke out in goosebumps and his breath came in fast whips.

"Do you think it was expensive?" Orion nodded toward the glass ball, looking worried.

I knew why he was asking. For months Orion had been

saving up for a high-tech robotics construction kit. He wanted to build a Mars rover to impress his dad. It was the one thing they shared—a passion for space.

"If we tell him it was an accident . . . that the metal was rusted anyway . . ." I trailed off, thinking of the rumors I'd heard about Mr. Vogelman. They were like stories of monsters that I only believed when it was dark and I was all alone. But now, walking up that dark, overgrown driveway, toward that run-down house . . .

"Do you think he really collects teeth?" Orion asked.

"Nope," I lied, trying to convince myself as much as Orion. "I don't believe those stories at all."

I wanted to sound certain. But the only thing I knew for sure was that Mr. Vogelman had an accent from somewhere else and that he often walked up Rock Street with a trash bag trailing behind him. How did I know that bag wasn't full of teeth?

Just then the house came into view. Orion stopped and let go of the ball. I lurched under the sudden weight.

"I saw a curtain twitch." He pointed to an upper-story window with a shaky hand.

"Nah, it was nothing." I had to calm him.

But Orion's breath was hitching, and his hand clutched the inhaler always in his pocket. I watched closely, ready to leap into action if his breathing got too ragged. Orion had suffered asthma attacks for as long as I could remember. Usually they weren't bad. Usually his inhaler fixed it. The important thing was to stay calm. I kept the conversation breezy.

"C'mon, I'm gonna drop this thing."

Orion didn't budge.

"You got your inhaler?" I prompted.

Orion nodded, then pulled it out, put it to his lips, and sucked in. I waited for his breathing to even out, which it did, but only for a moment. As he stared at the house, the wheezing started again.

"Don't worry," I joked. "I'll do all the talking."

Orion didn't laugh, even though he knew I didn't talk to strangers—or more accurately, *couldn't*. Kids were usually OK, but adults? No way. And a bunch of people all at once? Never in a gazillion years. When I tried to speak to strangers, my throat closed up and I choked on my words.

I'd been seeing a speech therapist, Mr. Carson, since I was four—two years after the operation to drain the fluid from my ears. I'd had one ear infection after the other for the first two years of my life. The surgery was supposed to fix things, but Mr. Carson said I'd missed "crucial phonological information," which basically meant that because I couldn't hear, I couldn't speak.

Although Mr. Carson insisted I'd improved, I hated

that I couldn't make my sounds match everyone else's. That's part of what I loved about art. When I drew, I didn't need words. Pictures were a language everyone understood.

I set down the ball. Orion caught my arm, his eyes widening.

"It's OK. I'll take the ball back. You stay here."

He gave me a relieved, grateful look and pulled in a smoother breath. I picked up the ball, keeping the crack side down, and crunched up the drive. This wasn't a hospital-level attack, so I felt OK leaving Orion, but I slumped low to show him how heavy the ball was. I'd do this for him, but I wanted him to know it was a hard thing.

"Pain," I moaned.

He gave a faint smile and took another puff from his inhaler.

"Suffering!" I laid it on thick. I'd been thinking up new ways to suffer all summer, ever since Aunt Lindy had given me a book about tortured artists for my birthday in June. They'd all had nervous breakdowns or tried to kill themselves. Van Gogh had even cut off his own ear. Clearly you had to be tortured in order to be a real artist. Problem was, my life was normal—no death, no torture, not even a divorce. Sure, I had a mean older sister and a baby brother who got all the attention, but that didn't count.

Speaking was my only true suffering.

Suddenly I stopped, struck by inspiration. That was it.

Maybe if I put myself into situations where I had to do hard things—not just the hard things I did for Orion, but *really* hard things, *every* hard thing, all the things that made me close my mouth and quake inside—if I did *those* things, maybe I would suffer enough to be a real artist.

My shoulders and neck strained against the weight, but I made it to the doorstep and eased the ball down. I was going to do it—the hardest thing I could think of.

I was going to speak to a stranger.

Chapter 2

I reached out my fist and knocked—once, twice, three times. As the echo of my final knock died away, my throat tightened and my tongue swelled.

What was I thinking? I can't do this. I'll start suffering tomorrow, I decided.

Quickly I dug into my pocket for the mini sketchpad and pencil I always carried. I scribbled an apology and a sketch of a hand holding out a spray of wildflowers, dirt still clinging to the roots. I hoped it said what my note didn't.

From inside I heard footsteps. I was almost out of time. I signed my name and Orion's and wedged the note under the ball. But before I could make my getaway, the bolt went *clunk* and the door creaked open.

I straightened to see a flowered apron, feather duster, and a square face with an angry mole against the side of the nose. This was not Mr. Vogelman. I thought he lived alone, so who was this?

"Ja?" said the woman.

I didn't breathe.

The woman looked me up and down, her eyes landing on the glass ball at my feet. With a gasp, she fell to her knees. She rolled the ball over, examining the crack, then glared at me as if I'd dropped her baby on its head. Cradling the ball in her arms, she turned and lumbered down the hallway.

I stood on the doorstep, wondering if I should close the door. I wanted to run down the dark drive and out into the sunlit street. I picked up my note.

Does it count as a confession if she doesn't read it? I thought.

Before I could decide, the woman called to me from inside the house. "You come," she said without turning.

I froze. I could say sorry. Just one word. That was confession enough for me. One word. I could do this. It was simple. My breath rose, my mouth opened, but my throat squeezed tight. I couldn't utter a sound.

"Come," the woman said again.

What could I do? I stepped through the door and followed her down the hallway and into a high-ceilinged living room with white walls and sleek furniture.

I could hardly believe I was in old Mr. Vogelman's house. All the neighborhood kids would freak when they found out. Orion would think I was brave. But I didn't feel brave. I couldn't do the hardest thing. Not even close.

The woman tipped the ball into a chair and gave it a little pat before addressing me. "You *vait* here."

Minutes ticked by. I breathed in to the count of ten like Mr. Carson had taught me, then out to the count of ten.

That's when I saw the painting hanging above the sofa. That's when everything changed.

The painting was humongous—as long as the couch. It wasn't a picture of anything recognizable but a great swirl of blue and black and white. Other colors too—little flecks of red and orange. Like a whirlpool, it drew me in.

As I crept closer, I noticed that the painting wasn't flat. Somehow, the surface had been built up and painted over, like the Cascade Mountain range that we papier-mâchéd onto cardboard in the third grade.

I'd never seen anything like it. It made me feel small, like when I looked at the stars, but also powerful, like stardust was swirling down to me. I wanted to reach out and touch it.

"Twenty-five years since I painted *dat* one and still I don't tire of it," a heavily accented voice said behind me.

I spun around as if I'd been caught with my hand in the

cookie jar. Mr. Vogelman stood in the doorway, leaning on a cane. He wore coveralls spattered with paint. His hair was fine and white, and one of his eyes drooped and drifted as if looking for a lost something. It took a moment to register what he'd said.

"*You* painted—" I was halfway through the sentence before my tongue flopped to a stop. I could hardly believe I had spoken. To an old, spooky-eyed stranger. A stranger who was apparently a real artist.

Mr. Vogelman regarded my gaping mouth, then smiled and aimed his attention at the painting. "It is the only one I could never part *vit*."

I turned back to the painting too. With my eyes on the canvas, I felt calm. I might be able to speak again.

Then Mr. Vogelman noticed the glass ball sitting on the chair. "*Vat* happened here?"

Or maybe not.

He set his cane aside to heft the ball. My throat squeezed tight as he ran a finger over the crack. In a moment, I knew, he would raise his eyes to mine and demand an answer. That's what always happened with adults. That's what made my voice burrow deeper.

But when Mr. Vogelman raised his eyes, it was to gaze at the painting, not me. It was as if the time and the silence didn't matter.

I was grateful he didn't press me. He didn't know that the harder people pressed, the deeper my voice burrowed. He didn't know there were parts of me that had been broken from birth.

Eventually, instead of burrowing, my voice rose to the surface. My throat relaxed, and a light bubble of sound popped out of my mouth.

"Um . . . ," I said, surprising myself.

Mr. Vogleman turned to me as if there was nothing odd about the long silence, nothing strange about the pause while I groped for words.

"Uh . . . we were playing, sir, and accidentally . . ."

"Old I may be," Mr. Vogelman interrupted with a laugh, "but I am not the kind of man who is a *sir*." He sat down with the ball in his lap. One leg jutted out to the side, and he winced when he tried to bend the knee. "Now *vat* are we going to do about *dis*?" He thumped the ball, and it let out a dull *ting*.

"Is it very . . . valuable?" I thought of the square woman's glare.

"Frouke *vill* be upset," he said. "I am not so concerned."

I kept looking to the painting, as if the answers swirled in its center. I wanted to stand there and look at it forever. And when I was done looking, I wanted to do it myself. I wanted to make art like that.

"Still," he said, "you *vill* have to pay."

"How much?" I asked. I had some money saved up. Orion and I could split the payment. That way he wouldn't have to use all of his robotics kit money.

I didn't look at Mr. Vogelman as I waited for his answer, hoping it wouldn't be too much. I kept my eyes on the painting.

"You know how to flatter an old man," he said. "You admire my painting. Perhaps we can work out a trade."

"What kind of trade?" With each sentence I spoke, it became easier. I turned to him.

A smile twitched at the corner of his mouth, and he pointed to the spray of flowers I'd drawn on the note still in my hand.

"You like to draw?"

I shrugged, suddenly shy.

"You do or you do not," Mr. Vogelman said sharply. "I have no time for in between."

I looked him in the eyes—both the straight and the droopy one—and saw that there was nothing scary about him. He was just an old man—a little cranky and a little sad. And he was a real artist.

I gathered my courage and my breath. My words came out a whisper. "I love to draw."

"Good, then you *vill* work for me. You *vill* start next

week Thursday. You *vill* help an old man with his art, and I *vill* forget about *dis*." Again he thumped the ball, making it *ting*.

The *ting* went into me and boinged around, touching every part of me. I couldn't believe it. A real artist wanted my help! This was more gift than punishment. And I had done the hardest thing—I had spoken to a stranger!

I felt very grown up and accomplished as I held out my hand to shake his. "It's a deal."

Orion was still standing there, tying knots, when I skipped back down the driveway.

"You made it," he said.

"I did." I held it all in, like a jack-in-the-box, waiting for him to turn the handle and ask what happened. I had spoken to a stranger! One all the kids were scared of! The triumph must be beaming out of me.

But Orion didn't see it. He held out the rope, studded with knots. Usually he tied messy, complicated knots that took forever to untangle, but these were easy.

I didn't want his thank you. I wanted his attention. I wanted nail biting, disbelief, wonder, admiration. I wanted to surprise him by saying that I'd taken care of paying for the damages.

But Orion didn't say a thing. He was ruining it.

"You're welcome." I snatched the rope from him and stomped down the drive. Normally I worked carefully, one loop at a time, but now my fingers fought with the knots.

We were almost to my house, and Orion still hadn't said a word.

"Aren't you going to ask what happened?"

He shrugged. "I figured you'd tell me when you were ready."

That really got to me. Did Orion think it had been easy for me—to speak, to confess? He was supposed to be my best friend. Couldn't he see I was changed? I had seen an amazing painting by a real artist who I was going to work for! I flung the rope at him. It was more tangled than when I'd started.

Chapter 3

As soon as I slammed the front door, I felt bad about leaving Orion on the sidewalk. Sometimes he was so calm that it called up a meanness in me. Now I didn't have anyone to tell my big news. I used to be able to tell my older sister, Jordyn, this sort of thing. She was fourteen and had always looked out for me. But over the summer, Jordyn had changed. She'd started hanging out with new friends and scoffing at everything I did.

Feeling frustrated, I entered my room to find Mom's butt wagging out of my closet. My bed was gone, replaced by a crib. My clothes slouched in bags on the floor.

"Mom," I said, panic thinning my words, "what's going on?"

"Oh, sweet pea," Mom said, untangling herself from the closet, "you remember how we talked about you and

Jordyn sharing a room once Benny was old enough to move out of our room? I'd say six months is plenty old."

I stared at the crib where my baby brother slept. A lump rose in my throat. "You should have warned me."

"For Pete's sake, Clarity. We talked about it last week."

Only my parents called me Clarity. They must have been feeling mean when they named me. Clarity Anne Kartoffel is the worst name ever for an artist. In my secret imaginings, I'm named Monique Silverthorn, and I have sleek, wavy hair that I toss over my shoulder in a nonchalant way.

I was nine years old before I learned what *Kartoffel* means in German. I will never tell a soul. My first name is bad enough.

clar•i•ty *n. the quality of being easily seen or heard*

Yeah. People could see me all right, but easily heard? That was not a quality of mine. And apparently I wasn't too good at hearing things myself either. I didn't remember any conversation about sharing a room with Jordyn. Sometimes my parents talked to me while I was drawing, expecting me to remember everything they said. But drawing was its own language, one that spoke to me louder than English.

Just then Benny gurgled from the corner. He slapped a hand on my sketchbook and gummed a torn drawing.

"Benny!" I snatched it away.

Luckily, it was only my public sketchbook. I had two—one that I showed to people and one that I kept secret. My public one was filled with drawings of horses and celebrities. The drawings in my secret sketchbook were different. I didn't show them to anyone.

"Mom, look what Benny did!" I held up half of a rearing horse. A wet stain of slobber rode bronco-style.

"Get the rest out of his mouth."

I scowled but fished out three wads of paper pulp. Benny made another grab for my sketchbook, but I jerked it away.

"He ruined my drawing!"

"Well, maybe you shouldn't—" Mom stopped and took a deep breath, then picked up Benny. "Why don't you help me with the rest of this stuff?"

Mom handed me a box of my kid stuff with Mr. Ya-yo on top. He was a Benny-sized yellow bear, my present after the ear operation. Mom and Dad had thought I'd be able to talk right away, but it had taken months for me to even say "Ya-yo" and another two years before I could say "yellow" properly. Truthfully, it still sounded funny when I said it.

I scanned the bags of clothes, the desk drawers pulled out, the boxes of shelf items. Something was missing.

"Where's the stuff from under my bed?" I whispered. I kept my secret sketchbook there.

"Jordyn helped me move the bed," Mom said. "She probably moved that stuff already."

I stormed down the hallway and burst into Jordyn's room, box in tow. Tubs of my art supplies covered the floor. Heaps of clothes slid off my bed, which had been crammed into a corner. One sliver of wall space had been freed, but it wasn't even big enough for my art postcards.

I drew a shaky breath. There was no room for me in here.

Jordyn lounged on her bed, leafing through the pages of my secret sketchbook. The sting of tears gathered in my nose like a hundred tiny bees.

"You can't look at that!" I yanked the book away from her, and the page she was holding ripped.

"Chill, CT."

Jordyn liked to shorten names into letters—*CT* for "Clari-T" was one of her favorites. I used to love that she had a special name just for me. Now it sounded like she was making fun of me.

Mom stepped into the room. "What's going on?"

I grabbed Mr. Ya-yo, clutching him and the sketchbook to my chest.

"Nothing," Jordyn said.

Mom looked pointedly at each of us. "Girls, I hope you can be mature about this."

"I can," said Jordyn, "but I don't know about the baby with the teddy bear."

"I am not—"

"Girls." It was Mom's warning voice. I could see she was working up to a speech. Mom always complained about how busy she was. She rushed around the house with spit-up on her shoulder and her hair sticking up in the back, signing school papers with one hand and digging in the diaper bag for a pacifier with the other. But busy as she was, she always had time for a nice, long lecture.

"We're fine," said Jordyn brightly. "We'll finish moving CT's stuff. Take a rest, Mom."

"Rest? What's that?" Mom went away laughing.

Jordyn closed the door. "Sorry for invading your privacy."

I knew she wasn't sorry. After years of practice with Mr. Carson, I could usually recognize sarcasm.

"You'd better get used to it," Jordyn added. "This was my room first. I don't need you bothering me. Got it?"

I nodded the smallest possible nod. Before I started speech therapy, Jordyn had been the one who spoke for me. She'd read my face, my gestures, my drawings, and she'd understand. I didn't have to say a word. Now I was only a bother.

"Nice drawings," Jordyn said, holding up the torn corner and letting it flutter to the carpet. "I like the one of the birds on fire."

I was pretty sure this was more sarcasm, so I snatched up the torn piece and stomped out of the room. I hadn't drawn any birds on fire. Jordyn didn't understand anything.

The day only got worse from there.

Mom made me fold towels in the living room before I could have screen time. Then, when Dad came home from work, he ruffled a hand through my hair and said, "Sorry about your painting course, kiddo."

I looked up, startled. "What about it?"

"Oops! I thought—"

"Way to go, Slick." Mom came in from the kitchen and passed Benny off to Dad. "I haven't told her yet."

"Told me what?" I balled up the dish towel I was holding.

"It's all yours," Mom said to Dad. "I've got to finish dinner."

"So . . ." Dad puffed out his cheeks, and Benny patted them, giggling at the scratchy feel of the stubble. "You know how we got a new roof this summer?"

"Yeah . . ." I squeezed the towel-ball tighter.

"And how your mother's not going back to work just yet?"

"Yup."

Dad set Benny down on the floor. "Things are tight. You can understand that."

Benny immediately started crying, so Dad had to toss him in the air a couple of times to make him happy again. I *could* understand, but I didn't want to. I didn't like where this was heading.

"We've had to postpone your painting course."

"But I've been looking forward to it all summer!" I felt like crying too. I felt like bawling. But no one was going to throw me in the air to make me happy. "That's just great. Does anybody in this family care about me at all?"

Dad made one of his sad clown faces. He should have been a comedian for all the crazy faces he made. Except this joke wasn't funny.

"We all care about you."

"Speak for yourself." Jordyn sauntered in to grab her phone off the charger.

"Jordyn, you're not helping."

"OK, I'll just go be unhelpful by myself."

"Take Benny, will you?"

Jordyn groaned loudly, but she picked him up and

started down the hall. "C'mon, AD, you old slobber bucket."

"Jordyn," Dad called after her. "What does *AD* stand for?"

Jordyn shot me a glare, like she didn't trust me to be on her side. She'd been calling Benny "the accident" since Mom found out she was pregnant, because it had been a surprise for the whole family. When he finally popped out, Mom made Jordyn stop.

"Say *surprise,*" Mom had said. "Think of your brother's self-esteem."

Jordyn had stopped . . . for a while. Then she'd started up again, shortening it to *AD*—Acci-Dent.

"It stands for A-Dorable," Jordyn said, kissing Benny on the forehead.

Dad turned back to me. "We'll sign you up for another course next year. When things aren't so tight. OK?"

I wanted to howl like Benny and run to my room, but I couldn't even do that because it wasn't my room anymore. It was Benny's.

"Fine," I said, even though it was definitely not. But I didn't want to cry in front of Dad.

I grabbed my secret sketchbook and pencil case and slipped out the side door. Lately it felt like our house was a ship. I could just drift away and no one would even notice.

Outside was quiet and misty. I sucked in great lungsful of air. If there was no room for me in the house, I'd go up on the roof. Mom didn't like me being up there, but Dad said it was fine before dark, so I climbed the ladder stairs to the sundeck and crawled up to the chimney, settling my feet against the grit of shingles.

From here I could see up and down the street. There was Mr. Vogelman's pedestal, looking lonely without its head. My eyes traveled the row of flowering plum trees—not flowering now, of course—that lined Rock Street. There was one tree where all the finches gathered. Everyone on Rock Street called it the bird tree. Why the birds chose that tree, I don't know, but sometimes when I drew it, I imagined I was there on a branch—a bird-sized Clarity—with bright chatter all around me. My bird-voice would be clear and strong.

Across the street was Orion's house with the grove of oak trees behind. My anger whipped up again. He was as bad as my family. Benny always needed attention, and Jordyn was at "that difficult age," as Mom was always saying. But what about me? If my best friend didn't even notice my heart bursting, then who would?

I flipped to a blank page in my secret sketchbook. Most of the drawings weren't of anything in particular, but rather shapes and patterns. They were drawings of what I saw when I took off my glasses, when the names for things disappeared, and all that was left was light and dark. All that mattered was pencil, paper, and me.

If nobody wanted to know how I'd actually spoken to a stranger and how I was going to work and learn in his studio, then I wouldn't tell them.

I pictured myself there, surrounded by canvases, easels, paints, and brushes. Mr. Vogelman had said I could begin working the following Thursday. Nine days away. That giddy, bursting feeling returned, and I slid a 4B pencil out of my case. The lead was softer than a standard school pencil, more easily smudged.

And so, as with any time things got fast and fluttery inside me, I bent my head, let my hair fall around my face, and began to draw.

Chapter 4

The next morning, Mom handed me a square of folded paper tied with twine. A complicated knot.

"Javier dropped this off for you," she said.

Javier was Orion's stepdad. Orion always sent a note when we couldn't walk to school together. Usually, it meant his asthma symptoms were bad that morning and his mom would drive him to school later. I shoved Orion's note into my pocket, annoyed that we wouldn't get to talk. I didn't want to stay mad at him.

"Hey," said Mom as I rushed out the door, "I think you and Jordyn will like sharing a room."

I didn't bother replying. If Mom thought that, then she didn't understand either of her daughters.

Two blocks from school, I ducked into the hollow of a large rhododendron bush to read Orion's note. I tried not to take pleasure in undoing the knot.

Meet me after school—I have something to share

P.S. You're the bravest person I know

—O

I crumpled up the note, threw it to the gutter, and headed for school. Why couldn't he just apologize? But half a block later, I spun around and went back for the note. I couldn't bring myself to litter.

Class had already started by the time I slipped in. Ms. Tink was holding up two fingers, her signal for silence. It was her first year of teaching, and sometimes she treated us like kindergarteners who didn't know anything. Other times she expected the impossible, like complete silence. Her frown deepened when I handed her my tardy slip.

"Litter?" Ms. Tink asked in her loud voice.

I nodded. It was what I'd written under "Reason for tardiness." I felt the eyes of the entire class on me.

"Please explain," Ms. Tink said.

"Um . . ." I gulped, glad that Orion was in a different class and couldn't see how brave I wasn't. My previous teachers would have conducted this conversation quietly, not in front of the whole class. But Ms. Tink made no exceptions.

I pulled Orion's crumpled note from my pocket and held it up. "Litter," I croaked.

There were snickers from around the class. Chloe Hoffstedder smirked, then followed it up with a look of pity.

Speaking at school was the worst. I didn't mind how my voice sounded around my family or Orion, but at school the words perfectly formed on the inside came out mangled and limping. Each year I had to work up to speaking to my new teacher. Individual kids were OK. I'd been with most of them all through grade school and didn't get teased much—anymore, at least.

"I hope you won't make a habit of it," Ms. Tink said.

I didn't respond, just slunk to my desk and tipped my head to hide in the cave of my hair. Out of the corner of my eye, I noticed the girl sitting in a chair next to Ms. Tink's desk—a new girl. She had a beautiful ski-slope nose and straight blond hair. On her feet she wore red high-tops.

"We have a new student," Ms. Tink said in her sing-songy voice. "Please welcome Elise Van den Berg to our class. Elise, why don't you tell us a few things about yourself?"

The new girl rose immediately. Every eye in class was on her, but she didn't shrink a bit. She gazed out over our heads to something beyond.

"My name is Elise Van den Berg. This is the seventh

school I've gone to. I don't expect it to be any better than the rest. My favorite color is red. I don't like to play sports. And I don't care if any of you want to be friends with me."

There was silence while Elise sat down. No one knew how to respond.

I was in awe. *What kind of person doesn't care about making friends?* I wondered.

"Well," said Ms. Tink, "thank you for sharing, Elise. I think you'll find many friends in this class." Her glare told us we'd better not disappoint.

Chloe exchanged a glance with her best friend, Poppy Jones. I knew what would happen. Elise was too pretty. They would either draw her in or cast her out. Like Mr. Vogelman had said, there was no in between.

Throughout the day, I watched Elise. Her posture remained impossibly straight as she sat at her desk, one row over and two seats ahead of mine. There was something fierce about her. I don't know why, but she reminded me of Mr. Vogelman's glass ball. Only she wasn't cracked, and I had no idea what swirled inside.

At recess I walked the edge of the soccer field looking at the sky. From the west, dark clouds coasted our way.

Across the field and up the hill, under the covered area where kids played wall ball and foursquare and basketball, Chloe and Poppy approached Elise. I was too far away to hear their conversation, but I saw Chloe flip her hair over her shoulder, then lean in and laugh. It was like flirting, except with friendship.

I watched with a heavy feeling in my gut. I hoped Elise wasn't like Chloe and Poppy.

Abruptly, Chloe stopped flipping her hair. She turned to Poppy, and both girls whirled around and walked away. Elise stood still, her chin tilted up. When I looked again, she was gone.

Chloe and Poppy could be cruel. I knew that better than anyone. Two years ago, when our class first started fourth grade at Walt Whitman Elementary, Chloe and Poppy had started by making fun of my frizzy hair and thick glasses. Before long they latched onto my voice, repeating everything I said.

I'd raise my hand in class. "I need to use the bathroom."

"I need ta ush da baffrum," they'd mimic under their breath.

I knew my voice sounded different, but the way they talked was horrible. I quickly realized it was best to remain silent.

But when they'd discovered I could draw, everything

had changed. Chloe would drape an arm over my shoulders and say, "You get to draw a unicorn for my binder cover."

At first I'd feared I was about to be the butt of some joke I didn't understand, but soon all the popular girls wanted my artwork on their binders. Kids I didn't know would beg me for drawings. I felt like a celebrity. Drawing had saved me where my voice had failed.

Usually, I kept to myself at recess, but today I wanted to find out more about this new girl, especially if she'd been brave enough to upset Chloe and Poppy. I left the field and climbed the hill to scan the covered area and the playground. No Elise.

I saw Orion in line for tetherball. He was no good at that game—too scared of the ball—but he kept trying anyway. I wanted him to spot me and run over to apologize. But he didn't.

I headed for the bathroom and pushed through the door just in time to hear the tail end of a sob. Then silence. Under the middle stall, I glimpsed a pair of red high-tops.

Now that I had found Elise, I didn't know what to do. I couldn't just stand there, so I made for the last stall. I slid the lock.

The bathroom was so quiet that I couldn't pee. I sat on the toilet, holding my breath, listening to Elise hold hers. I wanted to say something, but what was there to say with these stalls and locks between us?

The first bell rang. I zipped up and flushed. As the water rushed back into the toilet bowl, I heard a loud swallow, as if Elise was gulping down every hard thing.

I knew then that it wasn't true—what she'd said about not caring if she made friends. I knew she needed one.

I left the stall. If Elise came out while I was still in the bathroom, I would say something, I decided. It didn't matter what. I washed my hands thoroughly, cleaning under each fingernail. I dried them in slow motion. Like a sloth, I made my way to the door.

Elise did not appear.

The words from Orion's note taunted me: *You're the bravest person I know.*

Yeah, right, I thought as the door closed behind me without a sound.

Chapter 5

Elise slipped into class just as the bell rang. She crossed to her desk, but I didn't want to see her face pulled tight and her eyes puffy. I didn't want her to be broken. So instead I concentrated on the horse I was sketching. I decided to give him wings.

"We're starting our book presentations today," Ms. Tink was saying as she passed out books. The cover said *Anne Frank: The Diary of a Young Girl*. I looked at the black-and-white photo. The girl had poufy hair like mine.

"These will be done in groups of two to four." Ms. Tink smiled like a goddess bestowing gifts. "And you may choose your own groups."

At that, the classroom became a whir of eye contact and frantic negotiations.

Ms. Tink's voice rose above the chatter. "Each group will be giving an oral presentation with a visual component, which could be a poster or a video. You could do a play and make your own props. You could build a model or diorama."

Students began moving their desks together. I kept my head down, glad I didn't have to join the scramble. Everybody always wanted an artist in their group.

I risked a glance at Elise. Her face was smooth as glass. She had tucked her feelings back inside and sealed all cracks. Good for her.

I felt a tug on my desk.

"You can draw. You can be with us," Chloe said, scooting my desk into the group she, Poppy, and Amber Heisner had already made with theirs.

I winced at the unicorns on all their binder covers. I had improved since I'd drawn those. Even my current horse, with wings too small for his body, looked better than those unicorns.

"Get Lucia too," Chloe told Poppy. "She's good at writing."

I glanced at Elise again. She sat alone, not even trying to find a partner.

"Chloe," said Ms. Tink, "your group has too many people. Perhaps someone would like to partner with Elise?"

My heart did a little flip, like a tiny dog doing tricks. This could be my chance. Chloe swept her eyes over each of us. I tried to look expendable.

"Can we divide it up so that one person does the writing and one person does the talking and one person—" Chloe started to ask.

Ms. Tink didn't let her finish. "Behind the scenes, you can divvy up the work however you want, but every group member must contribute to the oral presentation."

"*Every* group member has to speak?" Chloe looked straight at me.

"Yes, every group member must speak."

Chloe's eyes darted from me to Ms. Tink. I always got excused from things like this—my parent would e-mail, Mr. Carson would write a note, and we'd figure out an alternative assignment. But something seemed to change Chloe's mind. Maybe it was Ms. Tink's harsh red lips pressing together that made her afraid to take the chance.

"Clara will go with Elise," Chloe said.

I got up. Suddenly I wished I hadn't heard Elise crying in the bathroom. It felt wrong to know something so private. It made us uneven.

Elise watched me scootch my desk next to hers. She didn't help. Her eyes fell to my sketchbook.

"So you're the girl who draws," she said.

I nodded, my voice stuck.

"There's one in every class," she said. "What's your name?"

I don't know what made me say it. Maybe I was getting better at hard things. Maybe I wanted to give Elise something private of my own. To make up for the bathroom.

"Clarity," I said.

Elise didn't laugh. She didn't ask me to repeat. She looked directly into my eyes. "Nice name."

"Everyone calls me Clara," I said, quickly.

"I'll call you Clarity."

I smiled, glad to partner with someone who took me seriously.

When all groups had quieted, Ms. Tink said, "Does anyone know who Anne Frank was?"

Tony Costello's hand shot up. "A girl!"

A smattering of students laughed.

"Yes," said Ms. Tink. "She was a girl. Do you know, Tony, when or where she lived?"

"Um, a long time ago in a galaxy far, far away?"

More laughter.

"Not that long ago, and not so far away, although it was across an ocean. Anybody else? Who was Anne Frank, and why should we care about her story?"

No one said a thing. Finally Elise's hand shot up.

"Yes, Elise?"

"She was an artist."

"Well, not exactly. She was—"

"Excuse me, Ms. Tink, but she *was*. An artist is a person whose creative work shows sensitivity and imagination."

Whispers rippled around the classroom. Elise didn't yet know that when Ms. Tink asked a question like that, she usually supplied her own answer.

Ms. Tink regarded Elise. "I suppose you could look at it that way."

Elise sat back and smiled like the *Mona Lisa*. Like she knew something we didn't. I wanted to know it too.

I looked down at my horse with his puny wings. Sensitivity and imagination? I scribbled him out—he'd never take flight.

"I was hoping, though," Ms. Tink said, "for a more specific answer."

"Oh," Elise said. "She was a thirteen-year-old Jewish girl who went into hiding during the Nazi occupation of Holland. During World War II. She wrote a diary."

Ms. Tink's nodded in approval. "Yes. Very good. Have you read the book?"

"No, but I've seen the play. And I've been there."

"Where?"

"To the secret annex. Where she hid with her family. In Amsterdam." Elise said it casually, as if she'd gone to the store for bread and milk.

I was impressed. Lots of kids had traveled—Hawaii,

Mexico, a cruise in the Caribbean. I'd been to Canada. But I didn't know anyone who had been to Amsterdam. It seemed exotic. But what the heck was an annex?

"Well, it sounds like you will have a lot to share with us," said Ms. Tink.

She could say that again. Elise was going to be a great partner. I tried to shoot Chloe a triumphant look, but she was busy looking bored.

"Open to page two-hundred sixty-nine," Ms. Tink told the class, "and we'll read the afterword to get the historical context."

I knew what she really meant—that *she* would read to us. Like we were in kindergarten. Next would be snack and naptime.

While Ms. Tink droned on about treaties and the German empire and Hitler and the Gestapo, Elise folded her hands across her desk, tipped up her ski-slope nose, and looked out the window as if she was following her gaze up to the clouds.

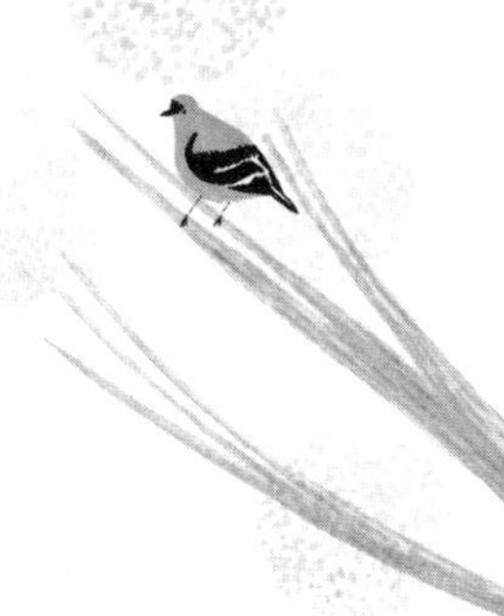

Chapter 6

After school I met Orion in our spot, at the special tree in the oak grove behind his house. The tree was so big and old that some of the branches swooped nearly to the ground, then rose back into the air before tapering to twigs. We'd played around, under, and on it since we could walk.

When I arrived, Orion was sitting on our regular branch, legs dangling. From behind he looked like one of those Norman Rockwell paintings. All he needed was a dog and a fishing pole. But his legs were too skinny and frail.

I suddenly flashed back to when we were seven and swimming in the creek.

Orion came up for air, and it was like he couldn't get

enough into his lungs. He stood in waist-high water, gasping and sputtering, eyes wide with panic.

But that wasn't the worst part. The worst part was that I stood and watched—watched the water drip from his hair, watched his lips turn blue. I didn't run up the bank for his inhaler. I didn't lead him out of the water. Everything in me went still. I didn't understand what was happening.

Only later did I realize the danger, when Mom and Jordyn come downstream. Mom scooped Orion out of the water and charged up the bank. It was only when the inhaler didn't work and Orion went to the hospital that I realized I should have done something.

After that, I made myself a promise: if a bad attack happened again, I would protect Orion.

I shook the memory away. But there were always crumbs of it left in my brain. I climbed up next to Orion. He was tying knots in a piece of rope.

He held up a fist-sized tangle. "Try undoing it."

"I didn't come here for knots," I said.

"Give it a try."

Great. I was going to have to be the one to bring stuff up. "Orion—"

"Wait. I'll show you." Holding either end of the rope

with the knot in the middle, he gave two sharp tugs. The knots disappeared, snapping to a smooth line of rope. "Like magic, huh?"

I would not be won over. "Magic—very useful."

He turned to me with serious eyes. "I'm sorry, Clara." He said it so simply. "I shouldn't have made you go by yourself. I know it was hard and I appreciate it. I'm not brave like you."

Just like that, I forgave him. "I'm not brave."

It was a fluke that I'd been able to speak. I knew it, even if Orion didn't.

"I think you are. To knock on mean old Mr. Vogelman's door like that."

"He's not mean. He's—" I stopped. I ought to tell Orion about Mr. Vogelman being a real artist, about speaking to him, about my arrangement to pay off the debt. But I was no longer bursting. "He's just an old man."

"About the glass ball . . . ," Orion said.

"We don't have to pay for it." It wasn't exactly a lie.

Orion let out his breath. "Really? He wasn't mad?"

"Not mad," I said. "He was—" I could tell him everything. Right now. But the moment had passed. Now it was a soft, delicate thing I wanted to keep all to myself. "He was reasonable," I finished.

"You talked to him?" Orion looked shocked.

I shrugged. "We understood each other."

"Well, thanks for going. I just couldn't—"

"I know," I cut him off. I didn't want him thanking me when I wasn't telling the whole story. It felt like cheating. "So what do you have to share?"

He looked at me blankly.

"Your note . . ."

"Ohhh," he said slowly. He fiddled with his knots. There was no rushing Orion into a new topic.

I took off my glasses. Branches and leaves cut the sky into pieces of light. If I squinted, I could blur the shapes, making the light stretch farther and farther until the ends feathered and fluttered. Having crappy vision wasn't all bad. I wondered if people with normal vision could see what I saw.

I swung my legs. Eight more days until I would work with Mr. Vogelman. Eight more days until I could see the painting again. My mind kept returning to it. It was like one of my secret sketchbook drawings—it was about a feeling, not a thing. I watched Orion's freckled face, his tongue poking out the side of his mouth. He would like the painting.

"C'mon," he said finally, hopping down from the branch. "You're gonna love this."

"A closet door. Big deal," I said.

We stood in Orion's house, tucked into an alcove under the stairs.

"Go in," he said.

"No thanks. I already know what's in there." That closet was so stuffed that things leapt out at you the moment you opened the door. Last time I'd gotten clobbered by a broken fan falling from the top shelf.

"You *think* you know," Orion said, "but it has changed. Trust me." He gave me a dopey grin.

What else could I do? I turned the knob and slowly opened the door. Nothing fell on me. There was nothing there except the smells of old man and split wood. No old-fashioned telephones, no broken tripods, no folding chairs. Just bare floor.

Orion handed me a flashlight. The beam illuminated the sloped ceiling and a larger space—like a cave opening—where the back wall had been knocked away. "Javier thought there might be space between the pantry and this closet."

Orion's mom, Mrs. Emerson, had married Javier three years ago. She hadn't changed her last name—she said it would feel like abandoning Orion—but Javier didn't seem to mind. He was the kind of guy who made a great stepdad. He was patient, not pushy. His smile was easy, not eager.

Orion and I ducked into the secret room and criss-crossed our flashlight beams over the walls and rafters. The room was narrow, like a hallway, with one side covered in peeling wallpaper.

"This"—Orion rapped on the far wall—"leads to the pantry, but they're not knocking it down until we start remodeling. So guess what?" The zing of excitement pulsed through both of us. "Mom said we can use this space until spring."

I had never loved Mrs. Em and Javier more. There was no room for me at home, but they had made room for me here. I could bring over all my stuff that didn't fit into the room I shared with Jordyn.

"Our own secret annex," I said, trying out the new word I'd learned earlier today.

"Huh?"

"We're reading about Anne Frank and the Nazis in class," I explained, a little proud that I knew something Orion didn't. Usually he was the smart one. "She hid in a secret annex."

"So . . . an annex is a space?"

"An extra space. Usually for hiding." That sounded good.

"Who will we hide from?"

There was no point in gloating to someone who didn't notice. "Our parents?"

"Mine already know we're here."

"We could hide from my baby brother."

Orion laughed, but I was serious. All Benny ever did was sit and drool. He didn't crawl yet, but he howled when he couldn't reach his toys. If I was home, Mom always made me watch him, but the kid was not easy to entertain.

Then it hit me. This could be the one place where I didn't have to be good or brave. Where I could be free from Benny, free from sharing a room with Jordyn, free from worry.

"Let's hide from every hard thing."

Orion thought about that for a moment, then nodded. "We can bring all our important stuff here. This can be our sacred space." I could see there were lights pinging in his brain as he warmed to the idea.

I nodded too. I already knew what I would bring.

Chapter 7

The next day after school, I dashed home to gather things for the annex. Jordyn was already in our room, trying on a tight sweater. She turned sideways to study herself in the mirror, probably checking to see how far her boobs stuck out.

"Is this what you do all day?" I asked.

She scoffed at me. "Grow up, CT."

I scooped up Mr. Ya-yo, my pencil pouch, and my secret sketchbook—which didn't feel so secret anymore—and went across the street to Orion's. With my foot, I thumped on the door. Mrs. Em answered.

"Oh, good," she said, ushering me in. She held up two blouses—one white with sewn-on beads and one black and flowy with bright color blocks. "Which one? I have to give a lecture tonight."

I smiled. Some adults talked to kids like they're trying

to make friends. Not Mrs. Em. She talked to me like an adult. I pointed to the black one.

"See, Javier?" said Mrs. Em to her husband, who sat on the couch, scrolling through the news. "The white is too conservative. Thanks, Clara. Orion's in"—her voice dropped to a whisper—"the secret room."

I nodded and headed for the closet door. When I stepped through, I gaped. Christmas lights and paper lanterns crisscrossed the ceiling, throwing color and light over the walls, two beanbags, and a little table.

"Welcome to Orion's wonderland!" Orion said.

"It's amazing." I nestled Mr. Ya-yo into a beanbag.

"Watch this." Orion pulled a string against the wall. The lights went out. Everything was dark except for a strip of light sliding under the closet door. "Pull the string on your side."

I groped until I found a dangling string. I yanked it, and the lights came back on. Orion had rigged each string to go up the wall and across a beam. There they attached to a pulley, went down the wall, and ended in a little hammer poised over an old-fashioned push button light switch. We pulled our strings, turning the lights on and off.

"Perfect," I said.

"All we need now are drawings for the walls."

I hugged my secret sketchbook to my chest. "These aren't for hanging."

"So, why'd you bring it?"

"We said we'd bring our most sacred things, didn't we? This is my real sketchbook. I've never shown it to anyone." Jordyn's snooping didn't count.

Orion nodded solemnly.

Please, I thought, *don't ask to see.*

He didn't. He said, "I know just where to put it."

Orion knelt in the far corner and stuck a finger into a hole in the wallpaper. With a gentle tug, a door the size of a microwave swung open, revealing a bare cubby a couple of feet deep.

"This is where we'll put our extra-sacred stuff," he said.

I fingered the corner of my sketchbook. I didn't know if I wanted it to live all the way across the street, but I couldn't leave it at home for Jordyn to snoop through again. Slowly, as if performing a ceremony, I slid the sketchbook to the very back of the cubby and closed the door. The wallpaper pattern lined up so perfectly that I could barely see where the door was.

We sat there quietly for a minute. I could hear the rain falling outside. But inside our annex, I felt bright and fresh as spring.

"I never want to go back home," I said with more force than I'd intended.

"That bad?" Orion already knew how mean Jordyn was to me and that Benny got all the attention. I hadn't told him the rest. Sometimes it took days before I could put words to my feelings. Now it all came pouring out.

"Mom's not going back to work, so they canceled my painting course. And they're making me share a room with Jordyn now, so that Benny gets his own room. There's no space for me at home. It's like they don't care. Like they're pushing me out."

It felt good to say it, but I wanted Orion to get mad for me. I wanted him to say, *That's so unfair!* But he only grinned and said, "You can spend all your time here."

"Yeah." I sighed.

Over the next several days, we brought more items to our secret annex. I brought my art postcards, my colored pencils, my chalk pastels—everything I wanted to keep away from Jordyn and Benny. Orion brought his knot box and an old book his dad had left behind—*Cosmos* by Carl Sagan. It was as big as a textbook, but Orion always said that one day he'd read it. He slipped the book into the secret cubby.

A few days before I was set to start work with Mr.

Vogelman, Orion hung a worn star chart from his dad onto the bare plywood.

"You should hang your drawings too," he said. "You should fill the walls."

"Soon," I said. This was our sacred space. The drawings had to be equal to what was inside us, like the star chart. That was Orion's heart hanging on the wall. And the *Cosmos* book—all the love he had for his dad was pressed between its pages.

What part of my heart could I hang on the wall? My secret sketchbook drawings were the closest thing, but I didn't have the courage to hang them.

As I crossed the dark street to my house that evening, I thought about showing my sketchbook to Mr. Vogelman. My secret drawings were like his swirling painting—full of feeling. But I didn't even know if I'd be able to speak to him again, let alone show him my drawings. And what if I was wrong? What if my drawing-feelings came out as garbled as my word-feelings?

My public sketchbook, I decided, was the safest bet. I had already torn out the mistakes. I imagined how my first day would go. Casually, I'd tuck my sketchbook under my arm. Mr. Vogelman would ask to see it. He'd flip through pages of horses trotting playfully. He'd pause at a sketch of Beyoncé.

"*Dat* is a lovely picture," he'd say.

"That one?" I'd say. "I just scribbled that when I was bored."

"You have talent," he'd say. "You *vill* be my apprentice, and I *vill* teach you *everyting* I know."

That made me smile as I walked into my house, the orangey light from the windows making it look cozier than it really was.

Chapter 8

Finally the day arrived. All through school, I bounced my leg in anticipation. When the bell rang, I ran the whole way to Rock Street. I hadn't told my parents about helping Mr. Vogelman yet—I'd been debating how to all week—but I knew I had to. Mom was big on transparency.

Mom was changing Benny's poopy diaper when I dashed in to drop my backpack and grab my horse and portrait sketchbook. *Good,* I thought, *she'll be distracted.*

I plugged my nose against the stink and said in one breath, "On accident, Orion and I broke Mr. Vogelman's glass ball, but it's all OK because we apologized, and I'm going to pay for it by working in his studio some afternoons starting today, OK?"

"Umm, well . . ." Mom reached for another wipe. "That sounds very responsible of you."

"Great! Gotta go."

I was out the door and down the street in an instant. I passed the empty pedestal and plunged into the dark tunnel of trees surrounding Mr. Vogelman's driveway. Showers of sunlight fell across the house. It wasn't spooky anymore. I couldn't wait. I was going to see the painting again—but that didn't happen.

I knocked on the door, and Mr. Vogelman flung it open.

"Don't come in," he said. "We do our work outside while the sun shines."

He didn't have a sketchbook or easel or paints or pencils on him. He did have his cane—and a trash bag, which he thrust at me as he shut the door. Then he noticed my sketchbook.

"You bring something? Leave it on the doorstep until we return. You will need both hands."

I wanted to ask him to look at my drawings, but my tongue floundered. I held out my sketchbook and stood there. Like an idiot.

"Ahhh," said Mr. Vogelman. "I see. You bring something to show me."

He plucked the sketchbook from my fingers and leafed through it, grunting as he went. My stomach felt like a million tadpoles churned inside. He frowned, then snapped the sketchbook closed and held it out to me.

"You leave it here." With a flip of his cane, he turned and crunched down the drive.

I stood there, dumbfounded. The tadpoles grew to bullfrogs. I hadn't prepared for this. Of course, I had hoped he would praise my drawings: *How realistic! What precise lines!* I had braced myself for criticism: *The hoof is not quite right. The shadow is too dark*. But nothing? A couple of grunts? Maybe grunting meant something in whatever language he spoke.

I guessed I had no choice. I placed my sketchbook on the doorstep and ran to catch up, the trash bag *kish-kashing* behind me.

At the end of the driveway, I caught up to him. Mr. Vogelman leaned on his cane and swung his leg out to the side as he walked. With every step, he winced. Unless that was his normal face.

I couldn't get up the courage to ask what he thought of my drawings, so I instead asked something else.

"Where are we going?" My words came out silky-smooth, exactly the way I imagined them in my head, the way Mr. Carson had taught me.

"Not far."

I thought of the stories about Mr. Vogelman and the creepy things he carried in his trash bag. "What do we need the trash bag for?"

"We gather materials. This old knee, she doesn't like to travel. The back is not fond of it either. That is why I need you."

When we reached the end of Rock Street, Mr. Vogelman turned up Amos, then headed over to High Street. Still, he said nothing about my drawings. The bullfrogs began to bellow.

I tried to prompt him. "I left my sketchbook on the doorstep."

"Good," he said.

It wasn't until we turned down Oak Street and cut across Clay that I realized he wasn't going to say anything unless I asked. Orion thought I was brave, but I knew the truth about me and courage: I was only brave by accident.

Soon we reached the middle school Orion and I would attend next year. Mr. Vogelman skirted the field where football players were slamming into each other. They looked so big and grown-up. I hoped Orion wouldn't get teased for being small and goofy. I hoped the older kids would appreciate him the way I did.

At the railroad tracks, Mr. Vogelman finally said, "We are here."

I looked around. The tracks stretched into the distance with blackberry brambles and tall grass lining each side. I didn't see anything special. "Now what?"

"Now, we walk."

"Huh?"

"Walk." Mr. Vogelman ushered me along with his cane. "You make this motion with your feet, yes?"

I didn't understand where we were going, but I didn't see any other options. I balanced on one rail, while Mr. Vogelman limped along the ties.

"There." He pointed with his cane to a small block of wood with two rusty nails jutting from it. "You pick it up."

My heart sagged. There was no secret studio in the woods. No perfect view for painting. He only needed me because he couldn't bend his knee.

"We're really picking up trash?" I said.

"Not every item of the trash," Mr. Vogelman said. "Only the useful ones."

At his direction, I picked up more wood and pieces of metal. I picked up nails, bolts, bottle caps, and colored glass.

"Careful," he said. "Do not allow the glass to free itself from the bag."

Smooth stones. A spiral of wire. A tangled net. All these things went into the bag. I didn't see how they were useful or what they had to do with art. Maybe Mr. Vogelman wasn't a real artist after all—maybe he was just a crazy hermit pack rat.

But then I remembered the swirling painting and how it

had left me breathless. My mind kept returning to it, stuck on how it made me feel—small and mighty at the same time. Only a real artist could have done that.

We kept walking. Mr. Vogelman pointed, and I stooped to pick up. Clothespins. A spoon. A jump-rope handle, the red paint split and chipped. We bypassed plastic bags, soda cans, and Styrofoam containers. The bag grew heavy. The sun sank behind the trees.

What did I get myself into? I wondered. This had to be some kind of cruel and unusual punishment for breaking the glass ball. I should have let Orion help pay off the debt.

Finally Mr. Vogelman announced, "We are done." He turned to head back, walking faster now.

"What do you do with all this stuff?"

He began humming deep in his throat. "I show you."

Chapter 9

"We shall not disturb Frouke," Mr. Vogelman said. He pronounced it *Frow-kuh*. "She naps, I think."

It took me a moment to realize he probably meant the square-faced woman who'd answered the door when I broke the ball. Was she his housekeeper? Or maybe his sister?

Mr. Vogelman led me around the side of the house to the door of a bump-out room. Through the tall windows, I could see rolls of canvas leaning in a corner and shelves stacked with cans of paint.

Almost immediately I forgot about fighting the bullfrogs in my stomach. I forgot about the frustration of picking up trash. We were entering a real artist's studio.

"Welcome to my atelier," Mr. Vogelman said. I didn't know what that word meant. He must have seen my confusion because he added, "You would call it a studio, I think?"

"Yes," I said. When he turned his back, I mouthed the pronunciation: *a-tel-YAY.*

Aside from the canvas and paint, the atelier wasn't at all how I'd pictured a real artist's studio. It looked like Dad's workshop in the garage. Tools hung on the walls. Lengths of wood leaned in a corner. There was a long, flat table, completely empty.

I searched for signs of a tortured artist—clutter, mess, some evidence of suffering. . . . I thought I would see it sprawled on the floor, flung across the ceiling, stained upon the walls. But everything was trim and tidy.

Mr. Vogelman leaned his cane in a corner, dumped the contents of the trash bag onto the work table, and began sorting. He opened a drawer and hummed as he worked.

"Behind you," he said. "You work on those drawers."

I turned to the set of wide, deep drawers. "What do I do?"

"Open the drawers, and it will become clear."

I did as I was told. The top drawer was divided into compartments of all sizes. Each compartment housed a different kind of object. Buttons in a square compartment. Wooden dowels in a long compartment. I pulled open another drawer. Forks with skewed and missing tines. Bottle caps. Every item had its place.

My task became clear. I grabbed a bent and twisted spoon from the work table and placed it in the spoon compartment. In the bottom drawer, I found a bin for the rusty railroad spikes we'd collected. All those trips up and down the street with his trash bag suddenly made sense.

We sorted in silence for a while. Finally, when I'd dropped the last bottle cap into its compartment, I asked, "What do you do with all this stuff?"

Mr. Vogelman regarded me for a moment, his normal eye focused near and his droopy eye looking far. "You would like to see?"

I nodded.

"You wait here."

Mr. Vogelman limped through one of the atelier's two interior doors and came back carrying a large square painting. But it wasn't a painting. Or maybe it was. There was definitely paint involved. Underneath the paint was the shape of a cross made from bundled sticks, untrimmed and extending beyond the borders of the painting. And the colors! Blue-green, like the sea. Yellow-white, like dirty foam. Flecks of turquoise and black. Dripping down from the underside of the horizontal bundle—rusty-brown paint, like dried blood.

"What do you think?" he asked.

I let out the breath I hadn't realized I'd been holding. What did he want me to say? It looked like he had glued a bunch of sticks on a square surface and splashed some paint on it. And yet . . . there was something about it—the simple cross, the bloody drips—that made me want to keep looking.

"It's nice," I said.

"Nice?" Mr. Vogelman seemed offended. "You think I paint *nice* things? My *vader,* he painted nice things. I make art."

Apparently, I'd used the wrong word. I felt my tongue fattening in my mouth, but I forced out some words. "I mean . . . I just . . . it doesn't look like a painting. Not like ones I've seen."

"Ah, now you speak some truth. You think this is not a painting?"

It wasn't like the painting I'd seen over his sofa, that's for sure. I didn't *like* it, but I couldn't take my eyes off it. I made a little movement with my head. Could have been a shake. Could have been a nod.

"You are right," he said, sounding more pleased now. "It is, and it isn't. I call it a relief collage. Some call it assemblage or found object art. It is giving new life to old objects that have outlived their usefulness."

Mr. Vogelman brought out more and more collages. Soon the atelier was scattered with works of art. His face looked like Orion's when he showed me new knots, like how I'd felt when I showed him my sketchbook. The memory of his reaction made me feel mean. I folded my arms and scanned his collages, grunting like he had done with my sketches.

But one piece stopped me mid-grunt. A cluster of red jump-rope handles spilled out from between two wooden blocks, looking like an open wound.

I moved from one collage to the next after that, forgetting to grunt. They were so . . . interesting. The kind of interesting that reaches inside and tugs the strings that make a person move and feel.

By the time I had looked at them all, my meanness had dried up.

"You see?" Mr. Vogelman said. "It is not about nice. It is not about liking or not liking. I make the art. And you respond to it. From here." He thumped a fist against his gut. "There is no room for pretty."

I began to understand.

It was already dark, and I had to get home for dinner, but I couldn't leave without seeing the painting again.

It was always harder to speak when I truly cared about something. Then the words and the feelings got all tangled up inside, and neither could get out. But I'd been visiting that painting in my mind for days. I *had* to see it again.

"Before I go . . ." My voice croaked. What if the square-faced woman was waiting to scold me about the cracked ball? What if Mr. Vogelman thought I was a bother for asking? What if the painting wasn't as special as I remembered?

I took a slow, deep breath. Mr. Vogelman didn't look at me as he stacked his relief collages, but something in the tilt of his head told me he was listening. With that small opening, I was brave.

"Before I go," I said, stronger this time, "could I see your painting again? The one in the living room?"

"Ah." His face lit up with a smile. "You make an old man's heart happy."

He took me to the living room, and we stood side by side gazing at the painting. It was just as I remembered—a great swirl in blue and black and white. But it was more than that. It looked like it was leaping out of the wall, coming right at me with that dark, pulling center.

Now that I knew it wasn't supposed to be pretty, I concentrated on my response, from the gut. I still felt small, but it also made me feel like I was being drawn in, pulled through a doorway to another world, a world that wanted me. All I had to do was lean in.

So I leaned. "What did you think of my drawings? In my sketchbook." My words hung in the air between us and the painting.

"You want an opinion?"

I couldn't say yes. I couldn't say no. I could only stare at that blue swirl. Even the bullfrogs held their breath.

"They are safe drawings," Mr. Vogelman said. "Very careful. You copy this, you copy that. You don't create."

All at once, the bullfrogs left the pond of my stomach. I swallowed hard. I felt like that collage, the one that looked slashed open with all the shiny red handles spilling out. I nodded and tried to say, "OK," but it came out as a squeak.

"Come back tomorrow," he said, "and we go drawing together. I show you how to create. We will not be safe."

I nodded but thought, *I should have brought my secret sketchbook. He couldn't call those drawings safe or careful.*

Mr. Vogelman hummed as he led me out, and each note pounded down on me, making me feel as small as a peg. I picked up my careful sketchbook off the porch and banged it roughly against my leg with each step down the drive.

Mr. Vogelman's painting swirled in my head, beckoning me to lean in. I wanted to. But what if tomorrow came and I couldn't draw? What if my hand froze up like my tongue? What if I couldn't create, I could only copy?

As I emerged from the tunnel of trees, the sky opened before me. I passed the bird tree, and the whole flock soared up at once. They didn't doubt whether they could fly.

As I watched them loop back around, I chanted to myself, "*A-tel-YAY, a-tel-YAY, a-tel-YAY.*"

Chapter 10

The next day it rained. Downpour then drizzle, downpour then drizzle. It was not drawing weather. Instead Mr. Vogelman acquainted me with his atelier. He showed me his pencils—fat and thin, in every imaginable size and color. He showed his brushes—flat and filbert, round and angled—some big enough for house painting, others with tips like fine baby hair.

I had thought this would be another hard thing—going back after Mr. Vogelman pronounced my drawings safe and careful. But it was like sliding into a warm bath that I badly needed. There was nothing to do but soap and scrub.

The hardest part was getting past Frouke. Her frown deepened whenever she opened the door for me, and she stood aside grudgingly, giving me barely enough room to slip through. I was still afraid of her.

Over the weekend, Mr. Vogelman kept me busy with sweeping and organizing. Mom had a thing about leaving notes on the whiteboard—more accountability—so every time I went over to his house, I wrote:

Clara —> work.

Technically I *was* working off my debt, and plus, it felt more important that way. I should have known Jordyn wouldn't leave it alone.

"You know, it's not work if you're just going over to your boyfriend's house," she said one day as I was leaving.

She thought I was going to Orion's. For Jordyn, everything was about boys.

"He's not my boyfriend," I said, but it gave me a funny feeling to even say the word.

At Mr. Vogelman's, I dusted and examined each can, tube, and jug of paint on the long shelves. I touched every woodworking tool, every sack of powder, every roll and tablet of paper, familiarizing my fingers with their texture and weight. When the time came for me to use them, I would be ready.

Monday afternoon I knocked on the front door as usual, but instead of letting me slip past, Frouke blocked my entry with her bulk.

"He is not here," she said in her heavy accent.

"Where is he?"

She stared hard at me, as if the force of her stare could erase my nosy question. "He come back Thursday. You come then."

"He didn't tell me."

"Who are you that he tell you *everyting*? Hmm?"

I opened my mouth but didn't have an answer. Frouke was right. I was just a kid working off a debt. Mr. Vogelman was a busy artist. He probably didn't want me hanging around every day. He'd probably forgotten all about me.

I turned and walked away, feeling her evil eye on me all the way down the long drive. I walked as slowly as I could, just so she'd have to stand on the doorstep in her menacing pose as long as possible.

Tuesday it rained.

Wednesday it rained harder.

Thursday I woke up to rain pattering outside our bedroom window, but by the time I walked to school, the sun had torn an opening in the purple clouds. Maybe today we would go out drawing.

We had yet to begin work on our presentations at school. First we had to slog our way through the book and class discussions. We were supposed to be at the part where

Anne's family first goes into hiding, but I was behind in the reading.

"What do you think of Anne?" Ms. Tink asked as she walked slowly up and down the rows of desks, preventing me from doodling. "What kind of person is she? What does she care about?"

Chloe raised her hand. "Personally, I think she's stuck up."

"Yeah," said Poppy.

A little titter leapfrogged through the classroom, and people glanced in Chloe's direction. Apparently, I wasn't the only one who thought she had no business calling someone else stuck up.

"What makes you think that?" Ms. Tink asked.

"She's always talking about this boy or that boy and how childish other people are and how she's so superior. It's kind of annoying."

I would have said boring. Anne did seem a bit stuck up, but I didn't believe she meant everything she wrote. She sounded like she wanted to be grown-up already. Like I wanted to be Monique Silverthorn. But she remembered too many details to care so little.

"She gets better once she's been in the annex for a while," said Lucia. "She starts sounding like a real person." Lucia had probably finished the book already.

Like me, Elise never joined in the discussion voluntarily. She sat with her chin cupped in her hands and a dreamy expression on her face as she gazed out the window.

But unlike me, she found something smart to say when Ms. Tink called on her a few minutes later.

"Elise, what do you think?"

My heart pounded. I'd already lost track of the discussion. If Ms. Tink called on me, there would be tongue-flopping and throat-clenching and lots of *umming*.

Elise didn't hesitate, though. She snapped to attention. "It's smaller than you think. They make the annex sound big, with all these rooms, but really, each room is tiny."

"Thank you, Elise," said Ms. Tink. And the discussion moved on.

Elise turned back to the window, where branches cut the sunlight into pieces. I watched her eyes squint again and again. Was she blurring shapes as I liked to do? Was she stretching the light to make it feather? Maybe we had more in common than it seemed.

At recess Elise headed straight for the pull-up bars. She took off her sweatshirt and boosted herself up to sit on the lowest bar. Though we were presentation partners, we'd barely spoken five words to each other.

I watched from the shadow of the covered area as Elise wrapped the sweatshirt arms around the bar and tied a double knot across her lap. She gripped the bar with one hand on either side. She held her body straight. Her chest heaved. Then she fell forward.

Involuntarily my hands came up, and I leaped toward her. I thought she would crash headfirst into the bark chips.

But the next moment, she swung up and around. All the way back to her original position. She twined one foot around the pole to steady herself.

I stood there in front of her with my arms out, looking like an idiot.

She grinned at me. "Thought I would fall, huh?"

I felt dumb to have been caught watching her and dropped my arms. Denial would be stupid, so I said, "That was pretty cool."

"That was nothing."

Elise pulled the knot of the sweatshirt arms tighter. Then she swung again. This time, she didn't stop when she circled to the top. She kept going—around and around, picking up speed, her long hair sweeping the bark chips with each revolution, her red high-tops blurring like some weird propeller.

I felt my chest swell, as if I were witnessing something historic.

When she stopped, Elise's cheeks were flushed, and her faced was tipped up to the sky.

"It's like watching you fly," I said.

In a flash, I knew that's exactly what she was doing, spinning like a propeller. She was trying for liftoff.

Chapter 11

I ran all the way from school that afternoon and arrived on Mr. Vogelman's doorstep out of breath. Frouke narrowed her eyes and led me to the atelier, muttering in a language that sounded like gargling from the back of her throat.

"What language is it?" I asked once she had gone. "That Frouke speaks?"

Mr. Vogelman was busy pulling nails from a plank of wood. Each one came free with a loud whine. In the atelier, he didn't use his cane. Instead he leaned on the workbench, a stool, whatever was handy.

"Dutch," he replied over his shoulder. "We come from the same village. In the Netherlands. In the north. Where it is all fields and cows."

"You came together?"

Mr. Vogelman chuckled. "No. We came at different times. She is an old family friend."

Now for the question I really wanted to ask. "Where were you on Monday? I came to work."

He looked up with surprise.

Yup, probably forgot about me. "Frouke said you were away," I added.

He bent over the nails again. "Sometimes I go to Portland," he said dismissively.

Portland was the nearest big city—where Aunt Lindy lived. I knew it had lots of art galleries because she had taken me to some near her apartment. Maybe Mr. Vogelman had a show in one of those galleries. But Frouke's words hounded me: *Who are you that he tell you everyting?*

I guessed I wasn't anybody.

"I just finish," he said. "Then we go out drawing. Before the rain catches us."

I fiddled with the nails, anxious. I'd waited days to get to the real art, but what if the drawings that came from my pencil were like the words that usually came from my mouth? Slurred. Wrong.

Behind Mr. Vogelman hung a poster of a man wearing a huge black hat that seemed to fly up from his head. Peter Paul Rubens—I'd seen his name in my book of famous artists.

At the bottom was a quote:

"My talent is such that no undertaking, however vast in size . . . has ever surpassed my courage."—Peter Paul Rubens

Rubens's beard and nose pointed at me like a challenge. If I didn't have talent, I should at least have courage.

Mr. Vogelman laid down his hammer and wiped his brow. "Good. We go."

He glanced at the sketchbook under my arm—the horse and portrait one. The H&P book, Jordyn would have said.

"Not that one," he said.

I threw my hands up in the air. "What am I supposed to draw on?"

"Hang on to your horses," he said. He dug out a large tablet—much larger than mine—that flipped open at the top and handed it to me. The paper was thin and brownish, not like the clean white paper in my sketchbook. It didn't look like it would hold up to an eraser, but I slung it under my arm and followed Mr. Vogelman outside.

He led me through the tall grass at the back of his house and onto a narrow trail that scaled the woodsy hillside. We climbed and climbed, leaving everything behind—Benny's stinky diapers, sharing a room with Jordyn, Anne Frank. Even Orion. All of it stayed down there while we climbed up and up. I wondered if Mr. Vogelman felt that way too—as if he was leaving everything behind.

Was this what Elise wanted when she spun like a propeller? I wondered. *To rise above her troubles?*

Finally the trees opened, and we stood on the edge of a sloping pasture. We hiked along the fence until we reached a cluster of boulders. Up we climbed. I didn't think Mr. Vogelman could manage with his bad knee, but he clambered up before I could offer to help. Then we sat there looking out over the pasture. Yellow grass waving. A few horses grazing. Through the trees below, glimpses of town—the Dairy Queen sign, Water Street, the track at the high school. I didn't know what I was supposed look at.

"We are here to capture movement," he said.

I flipped open the sketchbook and propped it on my knees. Then I pulled my pencil case out of my sweatshirt pocket. Inside were my real artist pencils, sharpener, and pink pearl eraser.

"*Nay, nay,*" Mr. Vogelman said. "Try this." Between his thumb and index finger he held a straight gray stick. It looked like a pencil lead with all the wood shaved off—only shorter and fatter.

I took it between two fingers. It felt delicate, like I might crush it to powder if I held it too tightly.

Wind rustled leaves in the distance. Did he want me to draw that movement? If I were alone, I would whip off my glasses and plunge into one of my secret drawings. I would draw whatever I saw and whatever I felt all in a jumble, and it wouldn't be pretty, and it wouldn't be safe, and I wouldn't care what it looked like in the end because there were things inside me that had to get out.

But doing that while sitting next to Mr. Vogelman would be like trying to poop with someone in the next stall.

"Hold the vine lightly," he instructed.

"The vine?"

"This is called vine charcoal. You must be free with it. Do not think. Just draw."

He sounded like Mr. Carson, who was always telling me, "Don't think. Just speak."

"Do not be afraid to make a mark."

"But what am I supposed to draw?" I asked, looking around. In the pasture before us, there were three horses—one far away, one grazing midfield, and one twitching his tail at the fence and watching us with hopeful eyes. One of the horses trotted toward us.

"It is not obvious? The horses, of course."

I looked at him in disbelief. "But they're not standing still!"

"Exactly!" He flipped open his own drawing tablet and began to sketch, his lines sure and free. The horse ambled away, but Mr. Vogelman kept drawing, barely glancing at his page.

My courage sank. There was no way I could draw like that. Normally, I drew horses from pictures in books. I had a *How to Draw Horses* book from Aunt Lindy. It had taught me how to draw light circles for the main body parts before starting the outline. Later, I would go back and erase those stray circle lines. By now I could easily draw horses without circles. I knew what they looked like.

"Since you are so fond of horses," Mr. Vogelman said, "I want you to *see* them."

My hand still held the vine charcoal above my page, unable to make that first mark.

"I see them," I said.

"No. You only see what you expect to see. I want you to see them anew. Now draw."

I knew this would not turn out well, but the vine charcoal was so delicious in my hand. The grazing horse stood fairly still—I decided to start there. I touched the charcoal to the paper and made a smooth, dark mark—the curve of the jaw. The sound of the vine scratching against the page gave me shivers. Such a thick, lush sound.

I drew the swoop of neck next. I had planned it so that the horse would be centered on the page. That was something I'd learned with practice. I used to start horses that ended up hanging their butts off the page.

"Do you watch the animal?" Mr. Volgeman asked.

I looked up. The grazing horse had moved. His head was raised. I thought to wait for him to continue grazing, but Mr. Vogelman said, "This drawing is done. Begin another." He reached over and flipped my sketchbook to a fresh sheet.

"But there's still plenty of room on that page," I protested, shocked at the waste.

"You must not be reminded of the old horse. That horse from one minute ago, he is dead. Draw the now-horse."

I obeyed. This time the horse stood still longer. I drew the head, neck, the sway of its back, and two legs.

"Another," said Mr. Vogelman.

If it had been anyone else—Mom, Dad, Jordyn, Ms. Tink—I would have balked at such commands. But Mr. Vogelman was different. I got the feeling he didn't expect me to be good or perfect or correct. He only expected *me*. Because of that, I didn't mind the brusque tone. That's how he was.

I decided to try the horse by the fence next. Unfortunately, his head was in front and his body was behind, so I'd have to try to make it look like the rump was going back. *Foreshortening*, my drawing book called it.

When I drew a line that went too far out, I reached for my eraser, but Mr. Vogelman snatched it away.

"No erasing," he said, with a glint in his eye.

"How am I supposed to draw without erasing?"

Mr. Vogelman cocked his arm, and before I realized what was happening, he snapped it forward and sent the eraser sailing through the air. It landed in the tall grass just inside the fence.

"That you will have to discover."

I gaped. My beautiful pink pearl eraser! The horse moved to investigate, and I stood up on the boulder and shouted, "Get away from my eraser, you stupid horse!"

The horse sniffed where the eraser had landed, blinked slowly at me, then ambled off. I sat down and glared at Mr. Vogelman.

"Another," he said with amusement.

I bent my head and scratched at the paper with defiant strokes. After a while, he said, "Better. More interesting."

I scrutinized the dark slashes and smudges. It was the messiest horse I'd ever drawn.

"These drawings . . . ," Mr. Vogelman said, leafing through this afternoon's attempts. "I look at these, and I do not feel the horse. I do not smell it or hear it. You understand? You must draw the *essence* of horse."

I did *not* understand. Usually when I drew, I had a picture in my head of what I was aiming for—an eye, a hoof, grass, a tree. If I didn't get it right on the first try, I could erase or start over until my drawing on paper matched the one in my head. But how was I supposed to draw *essence*? And without an eraser? I didn't get it. Mr. Vogelman seemed to be saying that matching the pictures wasn't important. Then what was? I felt like a failure.

"Now"—he uncovered a fresh sheet and pointed to the horse parading slowly along the fence—"draw that horse. Do not think. Just draw. You have ten seconds."

"Ten seconds?"

"Nine . . ."

"A person can't draw a horse in ten seconds!"

"Eight . . ."

"But I—"

"Seven . . ."

Fine. It was impossible, but I'd do it anyway.

With a huff, I shook my hair back and drew as fast as I could. I only got an ear and the start of the forelock before Mr. Vogelman shouted, "Stop!" Then, "Again!"

I barely had time to flip to a new sheet. I started with the eye. The horse moved so much that I couldn't pinpoint any features.

"Stop!"

"What is the point of this?" I wailed.

"You are learning to see," Mr. Vogelman said calmly.

"Ugh!" I dragged an ugly *X* through my drawing. I missed my eraser.

Mr. Vogelman stopped my hand. "Never do that," he said kindly. "Every effort is valuable. We must not rub out our failures. They are most important to our success."

I tried not to roll my eyes. That was just the sort of thing my dad would say. Why did adults think it was so great to make mistakes? Nobody wants to make mistakes.

"I bet *you* don't make drawing mistakes," I muttered.

Mr. Vogelman laughed with such force I thought he might fall off the boulder. The horse startled, his ears flicking forward.

"Most of my first efforts are failures," he said when he stopped laughing. "I must fail nine times in order to recognize the success of the tenth try. It is the failures that point us to the right path."

I didn't believe him. That couldn't be true. Once I was a real artist, it wouldn't be so hard anymore. I was doing every hard thing *now*.

"Again!" Mr. Vogelman nodded to the horse.

I groaned. "But he's moving."

"Then draw the movement."

How could I draw movement?

"Ten . . . nine . . . eight . . ."

Feeling stubborn, I wasted most of my seconds glaring at the horse as it walked along twitching its tail. "Impossible," I said under my breath.

"Three . . . two . . ."

In desperation, I swiped a couple of marks down the page. There—a tail.

"Stop!" Mr. Vogelman shouted. "Ah, the flick of the tail. That begins to look like it."

Look like what? I thought. My sketch was barely a doodle. Two wavy lines with a notch at the top that hinted at the horse's rump.

"So, I can just scribble anything, and it's art?" I snapped. Something bitter rose in my throat. First, he'd thrown away my eraser, and now he was trying to tell me a scribble—one even Benny could do—was better than my "safe and careful" horse drawings?

"Is it only a scribble, or did you *see* the horse?"

I wanted to sulk and ignore his meaning. But that would be the easy thing to do. *I'm here to do the hard thing,* I reminded myself.

I replayed the horse's walk in my mind—the twitch of ear, the eye swiveling to meet mine, the bob and stamp that sent a ripple down the mane and flank, ending with a flick of tail.

My heart leapt. I *had* seen the horse. I had drawn that flick because it said to me, "Here I am. I am horse."

"I did see it!" I said, excited for more.

Mr. Vogelman's eyes shone, and I knew I had pleased

him. "Now you have the idea. We give you more time. Thirty seconds."

"Gee, thanks," I said.

"This time you will look only at the horse, never the paper."

I laughed.

He didn't.

"How am I supposed to draw the perfect horse if I can't even look at what I'm doing?"

"You are not here to draw the perfect horse. You are learning to *see* the horse. Before you can draw, you must see. For that, you have no need to look at what your hand does. It will only distract." He flipped the previous sheet of paper back up to cover my hand, which was poised to draw. "Begin!"

The horse was really moving now. I watched the way its flank jolted from side to side. My vine charcoal slid and scratched across the page. I tried to forget what my hand was drawing and concentrate on what my eyes were seeing.

All too soon, Mr. Vogelman called, "Stop!"

I had just begun.

I hoped maybe, by some miracle, my drawing would look as good as the picture in my head. But when I glanced down, my horse looked more like a hippo.

"The drawing does not matter," Mr. Vogelman said. "Did you see the horse?"

"Yes, I saw it," I said, impatiently.

"Of course, but did you understand it?"

I thought back. In those thirty seconds, I had noticed things about the horse that I'd never included in my drawings before. Shine and sinew. Force and life. I didn't know exactly how to draw everything I saw, but I wanted to keep trying.

This was hard. But I liked it.

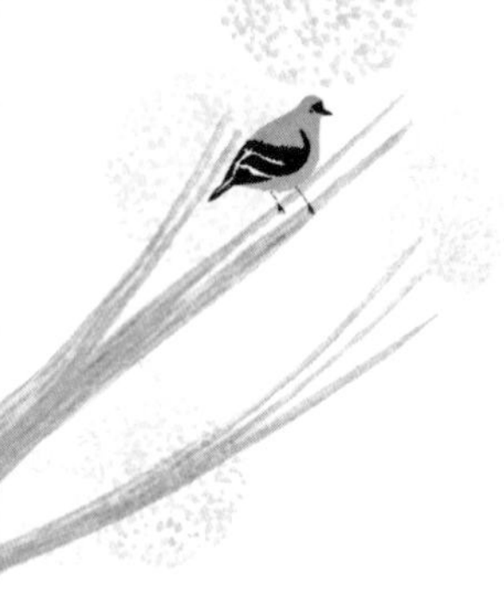

Chapter 12

Coming down the trail from the horse pasture was like descending through a layer of clouds. Back down to earth.

I slid into my place at the table just in time for dinner. Same old spaghetti and meatballs that Mom made every week. I stirred the pasta around on my plate, watching the movement and half-listening to Jordyn tell Dad about how Sophie Wilson was going out with Jason Spitzer.

"Going where?" Dad asked. It was the same joke he always made.

Jordyn groaned and rolled her eyes, just like she did every time. We'd had this same dinner a million times, with Benny trying to swallow his own fist and Mom forcing pea-mush into him.

Everything was the same. Only I felt completely different.

I wanted to draw horses again, but the rain returned and settled in. Over the next week, when I wasn't helping Mr. Vogelman in his atelier, I joined Orion in the annex. The ping of raindrops hitting the ductwork above was our own personal concert.

Orion had finally bought the robotics kit he'd been saving up for and was carefully sorting the pieces. His tongue poked out of the side of his mouth when he concentrated. I drew that. He wasn't moving much, so it was easier than horses. I focused on seeing his essence. We'd been friends since we were babies, so I thought there wouldn't be anything new to see.

But I was wrong.

When Orion looked up and saw me drawing him, he grinned that wide, goofy grin of his. But there was an extra-something that made me squirm. He was too happy.

"What?" I asked.

"Nothing." He shrugged. "I'm just glad, you know? It's nice in here. Just the two of us."

"Yeah," I said, feeling guilty. It might be just the two of us in here, but not outside. I had someone else now, even if he was a grumpy old man. And then there was my new project partner, Elise.

I kept drawing but avoided looking at my friend. Orion

didn't seem to need anyone besides me, but maybe I needed more than him.

Under pelting rain, the leaves changed color. They fell, clogging gutters and drainage ditches. Lakes formed at street corners.

I felt just as blocked when I tried to talk to Elise during small-group discussion. She wouldn't let anyone in. We were making our way through Anne Frank's diary, and as usual, I was behind in the reading. But I figured out that people in the annex were getting irritated with each other because Ms. Tink told us to discuss what it would feel like to share a small, cramped space with people you didn't know. And never go outside. And always be quiet.

Elise flipped through the book, her expression tight as glass. "I'd keep to myself," she said.

"What if you couldn't?" I asked. "Anne even had to share a bedroom with a dentist."

Elise's eyes locked onto mine. "Then I'd be mean so people would leave me alone."

For a moment it seemed like she was telling *me* to leave her alone. But then I remembered her sobs in the girls' bathroom. I wanted to erase that moment for her.

Maybe if I *tap-tap-tapped* on the glass, she'd know she didn't have to shut me out.

"Don't mind Chloe," I said. "She's mean to everyone."

Elise looked up sharply. "Who says I mind?"

A crack in the glass.

"I don't need anybody feeling sorry for me."

"I only wanted to—"

"To be nice to the poor new girl?" she snapped. "Save it. If that's why you want me as a partner, then go be nice by yourself."

"No," I said, "I want you as a partner because . . ."

All my reasons sounded corny. *Because you're trying for liftoff. Because you feather the light too. Because I want to be friends.* What I blurted out was equally corny. "Because Anne Frank *is* an artist. And so am I."

"Oh?" Elise looked surprised.

"And I think you are too." I breathed heavily from the strain of sincerity.

"Of course I am," she said as if it were the most obvious thing in the world. "Just not the same as you." She put down her book. "Look, Clarity, can I count on you for this thing?"

"What do you mean?"

Her eyes bored into me. "You don't say much in class. You're not going to be able to speak for the presentation, are you?"

"Oh, that?" I said. "It'll be fine." I made a mental note to remind Mom to get me excused from the presentation. I'd probably have to write something extra or give the speech to a friend. That's how it usually worked.

"Really?" Her eyes narrowed to slits.

"Yeah!" I tried to sound casual, but it came out too cheery. In truth, I didn't want to tell Elise about my accommodations. She might think less of me, and then we'd have no chance of becoming friends.

Elise was still eying me. "I'm going to need a pledge."

"What?"

"A pledge. It's more than a promise." She leaned forward. Her intensity flustered me, but it also drew me in.

"OK."

"OK, what?"

"OK, I pledge . . . ?"

Elise gave an exasperated sigh. "You have to say the whole thing. 'I, Clarity Kartoffel—here, I'll write it down." She bent over her notebook and scribbled furiously. Then she slid the notebook across to me. "Read it."

I cleared my throat and spoke softly, hoping I could get through the pledge without my words turning to mush. "I, Clarity Kartoffel, do solemnly pledge . . . not to let my partner down."

I paused. Elise didn't seem to mind my quiet tone.

Her eyes concentrated on my lips as if the words were a magic spell that would free her from a curse.

"I will speak in front of the class or die in the attempt," I finished. The weight of the words sank into me. "Die in the attempt?"

"A figure of speech. The important part is not letting me down."

"Class!" Ms. Tink called from her desk. "Please keep your discussions to the topic!"

Elise slid her book over as if she'd been studying it the whole time. "I changed my mind."

I felt a moment of panic. *About the pledge? About being partners with me?*

"About what?" I forced myself to ask calmly.

"About the annex. If I couldn't keep to myself then I guess I'd try to make a friend."

She sent me a sly smile. And just like that, a switch flipped between us. We were friends.

"Seriously, though." Elise leaned forward. "Why is it so hard for you to speak?"

I shrugged. How much could I tell her?

I was two years old before my parents realized that all the ear infections I'd been having were affecting my hearing—and my speech. Jordyn used to tell me the story when we were younger—back when she still told me things.

"Tell about the cookie!" I would beg.

We'd nestle ourselves in a pile of blankets and pillows, and Jordyn would say, "Mom used to try to trick you into talking."

"After my operation?"

"Yes, after the operation to drain your ears. Mom and Dad thought you still couldn't hear because you couldn't talk."

That part always made me sad. "Poor me," I'd say.

"Yes, but it wasn't your fault."

"It wasn't?"

Jordyn would shake her head. "No. You tried and tried, but your sounds came out different. It was like you had a mouthful of mashed potatoes."

I would nod gravely, remembering that feeling of frustration. It had never completely disappeared.

"Nobody could understand you," Jordyn would continue. "No wonder you stayed quiet. Even when Mom tried to trick you by giving *me* a cookie."

"But not me?" I'd ask.

"She wouldn't give you one unless you asked for it. With words. But I knew you couldn't, so I stuck up for you!"

That was my favorite part.

"I shared mine with you, like this." Jordyn would pretend to feed me little bites of cookie, and I could almost taste the sweetness, knowing that my big sister had taken care of me.

"When you were four," Jordyn would continue, "you went to Mr. Carson."

All I remembered from those early sessions was his sour breath. Later he had plied me with candy. I remembered rolling jawbreakers around in my mouth while practicing sounds.

"And then you could speak!" Jordyn would finish.

But it hadn't been that easy. At first I'd only spoken at home. At the grocery store, the bank, the park, anywhere with unfamiliar people, I'd open my mouth but be unable to push words past my tight throat and thick tongue.

With Mr. Carson's help, my speaking had improved. By first grade, I could talk to classmates. By second grade, I could talk to my teacher and classroom assistants. And by third grade, I was comfortable enough to answer questions in class—as long as I didn't have to stand up in front of everyone.

But I'd always felt two steps behind. Like I'd somehow missed what everyone else already knew.

I didn't tell Elise the whole story. I didn't tell about Mr. Carson or the jawbreakers, but I did say, "I had delayed speech. That's why my voice sounds like this."

"Like what?"

It was my turn to react sharply. "You don't have to be nice."

"I'm never nice." But the look she gave me was new. Like *she* wanted to see inside *me*.

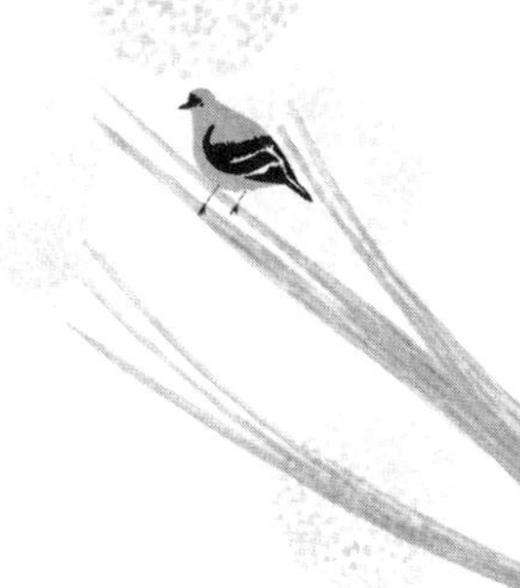

Chapter 13

October trudged toward November. Mr. Vogelman and I fell into a pattern of working every Thursday.

"I have no appointments on Thursdays," he said.

One Thursday, he showed me how to prime a canvas with gesso. The next, I helped him choose relief collages for an upcoming show in Chicago. I felt privileged to help a real artist ready his work for a show in a city as far away as Chicago! But Mr. Vogelman treated it more like an annoyance, something he'd been putting off.

On the third Thursday, he made me draw hundreds of long parallel lines down a sheet of newsprint. Then I had to do huge circles over and over and over.

"What's the point of this?" I asked, stretching out my cramping hand.

"It is like weight training for your art muscles," he explained.

"So, I need to have strong hands?"

"Not strong—steady. Your hands, your eyes, your brain. Those are what we exercise."

I groaned and took up my pencil. But I loved every minute.

The next week I tried coming on a Monday, to see if he needed help packing his collages for shipping. But Frouke turned me away, saying, "Not here."

"Where is he?"

"*Dat* is no business of yours."

What did he do, I wondered, on those other days when I hung out in the annex with Orion? I didn't ask. But every Thursday, like magic, Frouke would stand aside and let me pass, though her evil eye always followed me to the atelier door.

In mid-November, something happened that gave me a hint about Mr. Vogelman's past. So far I hadn't seen much of a tortured artist in him. Van Gogh had cut off his own ear. Gauguin had tried to kill himself. Georgia O'Keeffe had stopped painting for two years because of a nervous breakdown. What did Mr. Vogelman do? He hummed while he worked.

But I couldn't help searching for a hidden side. Some

tragedy in his past that might reveal his suffering. Sometimes he got that sad look and his droopy eye seemed to slide down his face, but he always shook the moment off.

That Thursday he was building a stretcher—a large wooden frame to stretch canvas on. I sat on the stool, holding the wood glue. Before coming over, I had been catching up on Anne Frank, an entry about bombs falling all day and through the night. Talk about tortured. It was bad enough Anne was cooped up in that secret annex with a bunch of people who didn't understand her. I knew all about that. But she also had to worry about bombs falling on her.

Suddenly I realized something: Anne Frank had lived in Holland. Hadn't Mr. Vogelman said he was from the Netherlands? Was that the same as Holland? He was old. I didn't know how old exactly but probably eighty-something.

I did the math in my head. He might have been a kid like me, like Anne, during World War II. Maybe Elise and I could interview him for our report.

Mr. Vogelman lined up the wooden stretcher bars in the corner clamps and held out his hand for the glue. I gave it to him and blurted out, "Were you in Holland during the war?"

He frowned but didn't look up.

"We're reading Anne Frank's diary in school," I explained. "I have to do a report."

He grunted as he tightened a clamp. "I was there," he said. "I was young."

I waited for more, but he only continued tightening and grunting, one clamp after another. I tried to think of something else to say.

"When I was little, I was afraid of thunderstorms," I offered. "I hid under this stack of blankets in the closet. I thought the noise in the sky would crush our house. Bombs would be way worse." I paused. In the book, Anne thought some people in the annex were cowards for showing their fear. I didn't understand what was wrong with that. "Do you have to be brave even if you think you're going to die?"

"I do not talk about that time," Mr. Vogelman said gruffly. He began to *whap* staples into each corner with a staple hammer.

A sinking dread came over me. What if something had happened to him or his family during the war? Something horrible enough to make his eye droop down his face?

Whap, went the staple hammer. *Whap! Whap!*

I knew I'd said the wrong thing. I'd missed the cues. Like always.

"I-I'm sorry," I stammered. "I didn't mean . . . it's OK . . . I mean, if you don't want to talk about it. I only wanted to . . . I'm sorry."

Mr. Vogelman looked up from the frame, and his droopy eye swung around like he just now recognized me. He softened. "Don't be. Do not worry about an old man wrestling with his memories. The war was terrible, but we survived. I was more afraid of my father than the bombs. I couldn't wait until I was old enough to come to America." He pronounced it *Ah-MEER-i-ka*.

I was relieved that he wasn't upset with me, but for the first time since I'd started reading Anne's diary, it felt real. Mr. Vogelman, a real, living, breathing person I knew, had been there. Anne's words were not just a story in a book. She was real. *All* of it was real.

Mr. Vogelman was still *whapping* with the staple hammer, each *whap* sounding louder and louder, like gunfire or bombs. He may have survived. But what about all the people, like Anne, who hadn't? My stomach twisted, and suddenly I had to get out of there.

"I need a bathroom," I said.

"Go," he replied between *whaps*.

"Um, where is it?"

Mr. Vogelman waved a hand. "Wander until you find it." *Whap!*

I stumbled out of the atelier and into the living room, stopping in front of the swirling painting. I always made a point of looking at it on my way to the atelier after Frouke let me into the house. Usually it calmed me, that feeling of being small but steady in the vast, chaotic universe. But today I felt unsettled.

I didn't know which of the closed doors led to the bathroom, so I chose one rashly, half expecting to hear Frouke's stalking footsteps behind me. She always shadowed me closely in the main part of the house.

I found myself in a bedroom. Half-closed curtains. Dim light. I knew I shouldn't go any further, but I felt as if a path had appeared before me. I had to follow it to the end.

I slipped inside and closed the door. The room smelled dry. Brittle. On the walls—only art. But on the nightstand were two framed photos: a grainy black-and-white one and a modern studio portrait.

My heart pounded as I sat on the edge of the bed and picked up the modern one. A young girl in braids. Her two front teeth were missing, and she smiled like she knew she was adored.

When I reached for the black-and-white photo, I heard a throat-clearing sound behind me. Frouke stood in the doorway with her massive fists on her massive hips. She was giving me the evil eye.

I tried to set the photo of the girl back on the table, but I fumbled. The frame went crashing to the floor. The sound of splintering glass echoed through the room.

I stared down at the shards, feeling like I'd shattered a sacred thing. The glass was cracked right over the girl's smile.

"I-I . . ." I couldn't get the words out.

Frouke rushed in like a thunderstorm, so mad she forgot to speak English. *"Je hoort hier niet! Ga weg! Schiet op!"*

I didn't know exactly what that meant, but I got the gist. I hurried out of the room and down the hallway. I'd nearly made it to the front door before Frouke grabbed my upper arm.

"No," she said with blazing eyes, "you must sorry *zeggen*." She thrust the frame into my hands and marched me into the atelier.

Mr. Vogelman looked up from his work as we entered, and Frouke immediately began speaking in Dutch. Her words were harsh, spiking up from the back of her throat. She snatched the frame from my hands and held it out to him.

"Kijk! Kijk wat ze heeft gedaan! Eerst de glazen bol en nu dit!"

I thought Mr. Vogelman would be angry. I thought

he would demand to know why I had been snooping. But instead he came around the work table and stood between Frouke and me. She was like a tornado, bent on destroying everything in her path. But she couldn't get past him. She kept arguing in Dutch, but I could see her winds subsiding.

"Calm down, my dear Frouke," Mr. Vogelman said. "It is only glass. Glass can be replaced."

"*Ja*, and some things can never be replaced." Frouke laid the photo frame on the table and gave me a hard stare.

Mr. Vogelman stiffened.

I took the opportunity to find my voice. "Mr. Vogelman, I'm so sorry I dropped the frame. I was only . . . I was . . ."

"I think it is best if you leave now." He rolled his eyes toward Frouke like she was a sister to be tolerated.

I let myself smile. We were in this together.

"But come see me before I leave for Chicago," he said. "I will be gone for two weeks."

I nodded. I would miss him while he was gone, but maybe Frouke and I needed a break from each other.

Outside I walked down the driveway in the drizzling rain. I passed the empty pedestal and the bird tree where no finches gathered. Only a few leaves still clung to their branches.

Just before Frouke had hauled me out of the bedroom, I'd glimpsed the second photograph. It was old and tinged brown. A man and his teenage son stood in front of a modest brick house. The father's hand was clamped tight round the boy's shoulder. Neither smiled.

But the boy in the photo—I knew his eyes. No droop, but impatience, like he couldn't wait for the photo to be taken so he could move on.

Chapter 14

One week before Thanksgiving break, we were still making our way through the diary.

"Skip ahead," Elise whispered to me in class. "It's getting to the romantic part." She grabbed my book and flipped past the February entries, right into March. "There!"

I read about Anne's first stirrings of feelings for Peter, the only boy in the annex. But she worried that her sister liked him too.

It's just like sixth grade, I thought. Girls were always talking about who liked who and who *couldn't* like who because somebody else already liked him or her. It partly mystified me and partly excited me. It seemed like yet another language I couldn't speak.

During class discussion time, Ms. Tink called on me. "Clara, what do you think?"

I got all red in the face and looked down at my desk.

I knew Mom had e-mailed Ms. Tink about my speaking difficulties. *Why is she still calling on me?* I thought.

Ms. Tink waited with a patient, encouraging smile, but everyone was staring at me and I couldn't even remember the question, let alone mutter a single word. Finally she said, "Anyone else?" and moved on.

I let out my breath. But I had the feeling Ms. Tink wouldn't just forget.

Elise cast a worried glance in my direction, and I could tell what she was thinking: *If Clarity can't speak now, how is she going to do it during our presentation?*

I gave her my best confident smile. Conferences were coming up. Mom and Dad would sort it out.

When discussion time was over, Ms. Tink gave us an assignment, due after the break. "This is your opportunity for creative expression," she explained. "You can draw a picture, write a poem, even sing a song. I want you to reflect on something Anne has been going through—the fear of being discovered, the issue of privacy, the possibility of romance." There were stifled giggles from around the classroom. "Or her relationship with her parents or sister. Whatever you want. Think how you would feel in her position."

More giggles from the boys, and Tony called out, "You mean if I liked that guy, Peter?"

Ms. Tink ignored him.

I already knew I would do a drawing, and a surge of inspiration hit me. I didn't know what I would draw, but I would do it in my secret sketchbook. It would not be safe and careful. The question was, would I have the courage to share it?

That afternoon, Mr. Vogelman surprised me with a newly stretched canvas. "This time, I let you gesso."

"Yes!" I grabbed a wide paintbrush.

He'd demonstrated priming a canvas before, but I'd never done it myself. I dipped my brush into the can of gesso—essentially white paint—and spread a long, straight stroke onto the raw canvas. The woven fabric soaked it up almost immediately. I slathered on more gesso, careful to keep all my strokes going the same direction.

"What do you need all these canvases for?" I asked. I'd never seen Mr. Vogelman paint on canvas before. His relief collages all began with a sturdy base—a plank of wood, an old cupboard door—to which he affixed his objects.

"It is good to go back and say hello to the old farmhouse."

"The old farmhouse?"

"Painting on canvas is where I began."

I longed to stretch and paint a canvas of my own. "When can *I* visit the old farmhouse?"

Mr. Vogelman laughed from his belly. "Your old farmhouse is drawing. You must see and draw, draw and see before you attempt to paint."

I sighed. It was worth a try. At least I got to gesso. I finished the last stroke and washed out the paintbrush. The canvas had to dry before the next coat, so I excused myself to go to the bathroom. I still didn't know where it was.

I hadn't taken three steps before Frouke appeared. "Something you *vant*?"

"The bathroom," I said, tilting my chin up like Elise.

"Come," she said and led me down the hallway.

She must have known that I really had to pee, because she walked un-be-liev-a-bly sloooooowly. I imagined a witchy smile twisting her lips. But when she turned in front of the bathroom, there was no smile. Only the same sour expression as always. Did Frouke *ever* smile?

The moment I had the thought, I knew I had to find out. A person couldn't be sour all the way through. It wouldn't be easy. It would take cunning and strength, but somehow, I would make Frouke smile.

"Every hard thing," I whispered to myself in the bathroom as I hatched a plan.

I stood to flush and found myself facing a painting. It wasn't like any of the others I'd seen throughout the house. This was a landscape. Fields stretching into the distance. A windmill. Cows. Harmless clouds. In the bottom corner, in small, black letters, it said *Vogelman*.

Was this what Mr. Vogelman meant about saying hello to the old farmhouse? I wondered. *Is this how he used to paint?*

Frouke stood outside the bathroom door, waiting to escort me back to the atelier, when I emerged.

Phase one: disarm her with kindness.

I said, "That's a lovely apron you have on, Frouke," and flashed my biggest smile.

She didn't flinch. Or blush. Or smile. The corners of her mouth turned down even farther. She said, "You do not impress me."

Phase two could wait.

Back in the atelier, I said, "I like your painting—the one in the bathroom."

Mr. Vogelman looked up over the rims of his glasses. But not at me. He was looking past me—way, way past. Like he was looking through the years to the time when the paint had first kissed the canvas, to when it was wet and could still be smeared.

"No," he said and resumed sharpening pencils. Curls of wood coaxed off with a knife.

"No what?"

He shaved faster. "No, it is not mine." Shave, shave, shave.

"But it has your name on it."

He sighed and straightened. "It is my father's, the only thing I have of his."

I held my breath. His father whom he feared more than the war and made him flee to *Ah-MEER-i-ka*? I had to know more.

"So, he was a painter too?"

The shavings flew off in short, sharp flecks. "I would not call him that."

I was confused. I'd seen the painting in the bathroom. "What do you mean?" I asked.

Mr. Vogelman took off his glasses and rubbed the bridge of his nose for a moment. Then he replaced his glasses, took up a hammer, and began to yank rusty nails out of a board. Each one whined high and mournful as the wood released its grip. Just last week, I'd watched him pound those same nails into the board as part of the piece he was working on.

"I hang my father's painting"—yank and *whiiiine*—"in the bathroom"—*tink* on the table—"to remind me what a painting looks like"—yank and *whiiiine*—"when it is"—*clink* against the other nails—"full of crap."

Thud. With that, Mr. Vogelman tossed the hammer down and walked out the side door, into a sunbreak.

I didn't know what to do. Was he angry that I'd mistaken the painting for one of his? Was he angry with his father, who was probably dead by now?

Heart thudding, I walked out to stand beside him. After so much rain, the sunshine made everything vibrant. Greens were greener, and the browns of fallen leaves were golden-orange. We stood with hands in pockets, staring at the vines overtaking the leaning gazebo.

"So," I said, just to be sure, "you don't like your father's painting?"

Mr. Vogelman let out a big, fat *HA*! "You could say it that way."

As we watched, a couple of Steller's jays rustled through the vines on top of the gazebo. One flew down to the lawn and back, then the other. Down and back, down and back. Like a game they'd been playing for centuries.

"My father loved the land," Mr. Vogelman finally said. "He loved the country, the water, the cows. He didn't love people or ideas. He was a hard man. I thought he wanted to clip my wings."

The jays squawked and flew up to the top of a tall pine.

I didn't know how to respond, so I said what I was thinking. "Do you like birds?"

Mr. Vogelman turned to me, eyes moist. "In my heart," he said, "I am a bird."

I thought I knew what he meant by that. It was like what I sometimes imagined when I watched the finches in the bird tree. When I could feel myself soaring up on wings of my own.

"And you are a little potato still growing beneath the earth."

Great, I thought. *He's a bird, and I'm a po—*

I wilted. He knew. He knew what my last name meant. If he spoke German, he must have known all along. The only name worse for an artist than Clarity Kartoffel was Clarity Potato. It was a round, lumpy name, not sleek and sure like Monique Silverthorn.

"How do you know my last name?" I asked.

"You think I don't know my neighbors' names?"

He had a point. *I* knew the names of everybody on the street. Why shouldn't he?

"The Germans say *Kartoffel,* but in my language we say *aardappel,*" he continued.

"*Aardappel,*" I repeated.

"*Aard* means 'earth' and *appel* . . . I think you make a guess."

"Apple?"

"Yes. Apple of the earth."

I smiled. "Apple of the earth." I liked the sound of that. Maybe I didn't mind him thinking of me that way after all.

"What does your name mean?" I asked. "Vogelman."

It was his turn to smile. *"En vogel"*—he pronounced the *v* like an *f* and the *g* like he was clearing his throat—"is a bird."

Vogel-Man, I thought. *Birdman.* It fit.

Chapter 15

"Mom, we don't call it a playdate anymore," I said as I hitched my backpack over my shoulder. Elise had invited me over to her house, and I was full of nervous excitement. We were almost finished reading Anne Frank's diary, but we had no intention of working on homework today. This was pure fun.

"Well, excuse me. I can't keep up with the lingo. What do you call it now?"

I was caught off guard. It wasn't really called anything, was it?

"It's just hanging out," Jordyn said from the couch. "Geez, Mom, why do you have to make everything a big deal?"

"Thank you for your insight, Jordyn. You can watch Benny while I drive Clara."

Elise's house wasn't far, but I was glad to have Mom

with me. I might not have found it. The chipped yellow paint and rickety porch were not what I expected. Elise was so self-contained, so perfect, that I expected her house and family to be the same. I'd envisioned a new house with chandeliers and napkin rings and *how-do-you-dos.*

"Are you sure this is it?" I asked before unbuckling.

"This is the address," Mom said.

Suddenly my mouth went dry. What if Elise had a big family and I had to talk to all of them? I didn't even know if she had any siblings. Why hadn't I thought of this sooner?

"Maybe we should do this another time," I said. "Don't you have to meet her parents first?"

Mom smiled. "I've met her mom at the grocery store. She's glad to see Elise making friends. We're pretty glad too." She leaned forward and kissed my forehead. "Want me to walk you to the door?"

I did. Very much. But that would be taking the easy way out. *Every hard thing,* I reminded myself.

"Nah," I said to Mom.

When Elise flung open the door, there was a hint of defiance in the tilt of her chin, as if challenging me to judge her.

"Enter if you dare," she said with a dramatic bow.

I waved to Mom and stepped inside. There was no

chandelier. Cardboard boxes lined the walls like Elise and her family were still moving in. The living room had only one thing on the wall—a poster of a kitten dangling from a rope with *Hang in there* written across the bottom.

I relaxed a bit. The house seemed normal and messy, just like mine.

"That's Evan," Elise said, stepping over a boy who lay on the floor playing with dinosaurs. "Mom!" she shouted. "Clarity's here!"

From the room beyond came the most beautiful woman I had ever seen. Though she wore an old sweatshirt and her blond hair was piled in a messy bun, she looked like a model.

"Nice to meet you, Clarity." She shook my hand. "I'm Charla."

My throat squeezed tight, but I breathed deep. I could do this. I had spoken to Mr. Vogelman. I had spoken to Frouke. I could speak to Elise's mom.

Charla flashed a smile with perfect white teeth and continued to look at me.

Just because she looks perfect on the outside doesn't mean she's perfect on the inside, I told myself. Elise had already shown me glimpses of her dark and mysterious interior. Maybe everyone hid a private mess.

"Hi." It slipped out, like a surprise burp. I was so

startled that Elise was leading me away before I realized the introductions were over. I had done it. Another hard thing.

"Rawr!" Evan said with his T-rex as we stepped over him.

"Rawr!" I said back, making claws with my hands. By the time we got to Elise's room at the top of the stairs I was grinning like a fool. It was like I'd been speaking to strangers my whole life.

Elise opened the door, her face shy and eager. For once she'd let down her guard. I felt as if I'd passed some test.

Inside, the room was painted blue, like the sky. It had a low, slanted ceiling. One wall was covered with a patchwork of pictures from postcards and magazines. It was a colorful, fabulous collage of images and words. There were even pages torn from books with sentences circled or highlighted.

I stepped closer to study the images of faraway places—the pyramids, the Taj Mahal, the Great Wall of China. One postcard showed a field of tulips stretching to the horizon.

"This is . . . this is amazing," I said.

"It's my dream wall," Elise said. "I have one in every house I live in."

Staring at the glossy pictures and doodles and thoughts and quotes it hit me—I was looking at the inside of Elise splashed up on the wall.

Leaning closer, I realized there was only one photograph of a person—a man standing on a beach, the clear ocean sparkling behind him.

"Who's that?"

Elise stood at the edge of the bed, arms folded around herself. "My dad."

"Where is he?" I asked. I meant was he at work, but as soon as the question left my mouth, I realized that the reason he was pictured on Elise's dream wall was because he wasn't pictured in her real life.

She shrugged. "Who knows?"

I didn't want to pry, but . . . "Do you miss him?" I asked. I couldn't imagine what my family would be like without Dad. He was the one who joked Jordyn out of her dark moods and kept Mom from stressing out.

Elise flopped down on the bed. "Never really knew him. He was always traveling. I used to want him to take me to all these places, but now I've decided I'll just go myself." Her eyes blazed with certainty, but there was bitterness in her voice.

I wanted to say something comforting, like Orion always did for me. "At least he took you to Amsterdam."

Elise sucked in a breath and rolled over to face the wall. What had I said?

"About Amsterdam . . ." She sat up and faced me, her back as straight as if she were presenting to the class. Her eyes pleaded, but I didn't understand why.

"What?"

"I didn't really go."

"To Amsterdam?"

"Or the Anne Frank house. Or any of it. I just said it, because, well, I never think I'm going to make friends. I meant to tell you, but honestly, I thought maybe you forgot. Don't be mad at me. I wouldn't lie to you now."

I knew I ought to feel betrayed or angry. But I didn't. Instead I felt giddy. Like I held a newly hatched Elise in my hands. Now I understood why she had acted so hard and mean that first day. She hadn't wanted to show her feelings, hadn't wanted to risk getting hurt. But she trusted me.

"I know," I said. "You don't have to worry about me. I understand."

Chapter 16

On the Monday before Thanksgiving, I spent the afternoon with Birdman, as I thought of him now. He was putting away his current projects and tidying the atelier in preparation for his trip to Chicago the next day. He would be gone for two weeks, which already felt like forever. Just when I was learning so much, starting to feel like a real artist, I had to stop.

"Maybe I could come and clean or stretch a canvas while you're gone?" I said.

"No need," Birdman said, laughing.

He seemed happier than usual and walked around the atelier as if his feet barely touched the ground. I squinted at the light from the window behind him. It feathered up all around his head.

"It's sad," I said, "that you have to spend Thanksgiving alone in Chicago."

He placed his hand on the top of my head. "Thank you for thinking of me, little potato, but I will not be so alone. There is a little bird I must visit."

"A little bird?" I knew he didn't mean a real bird. I thought of the photo I'd seen in the bedroom the day I'd gone snooping. The one of the girl with braids. I wondered again who she was. His granddaughter? He'd never said he had a wife, son, or daughter.

"I will tell you about it when I return. And I will give you an assignment to keep you busy."

Well, that was something. I had been drawing little things, trying to capture their essence. A cat in the yard. Benny eating his own toes. Paper clips and coffee mugs. But I needed something bigger. Something huge.

"You will have to look harder than you've ever looked before," Birdman said. "You will have to persevere. You will have to do it all alone."

"OK." I was ready. *Every hard thing,* I thought. I imagined huge canvases. Fireworks. Volcanoes. Comets.

"You must draw one thing."

"One thing," I repeated. "Give it to me."

"Choose something in nature that you can visit often. A tree would be good. You must draw that one tree."

"And . . . ?" I prompted. "What else?"

"That is it," Birdman said. "One tree."

"One drawing of a tree? That's it? That won't take two weeks!"

"Ah, but I did not say one drawing. I said one tree. You are to keep drawing the tree until you understand it."

"So a couple of drawings?"

Birdman's droopy eye swung around. "More than that, I should think."

"Five or six?"

"Fifty might be enough," he said mildly.

My mouth fell open. "Fifty?"

"Then again, it may require one hundred."

"A hundred drawings of one tree?" That wasn't huge. It was boring.

"Only you will know when you have understood."

"But it's rainy and cold," I protested. "How can I draw outside? My sketchbook will get soaked."

Birdman headed out of the atelier and down the hallway to where his suitcase waited by the door. He gave a wave of his cane. "You will think of something."

I wasn't so sure. But then I thought of Orion. For the past two weeks in the annex, he'd been frustrated that the online instructions he'd found for building a Mars rover weren't working. He would love the challenge of rigging up a rain shelter.

"So," I said, "it's possible that I could understand after only twenty drawings?"

"It is possible. You will show me when you finish. The drawings will tell the truth."

I sighed. Forget about two weeks—I'd be drawing one tree for the rest of my life.

"After you have done this, it will be time to paint."

My heart forgot to thump. "With real artist paint?"

"Yes." Birdman laughed. "And real brushes."

If it meant getting to paint, I would draw one tree while doing somersaults. I already had one picked out—the swooping oak behind Orion's house.

Chapter 17

I didn't start the assignment right away. First my parents had to ruin my life.

While Birdman's plane flew over the Rockies and the plains of the Midwest, Mom and Dad came home from parent-teacher conferences. Usually conferences were the same old story. I struggled with reading and spelling and social interactions. Jordyn needed to work on her attitude. But this time they sat me down and sent Jordyn away with Benny.

"We talked to your teacher tonight, Clara," Mom began, "and we all agree that you are ready to challenge yourself."

I nodded like I agreed. Grown-ups always wanted kids to challenge themselves. But I was already doing every hard thing. What more did they want?

"And Mr. Carson says you barely need him anymore," Dad added.

I stopped nodding. Something about Dad's tight smile and Mom's deliberate calm worried me. And why were they bringing up my speech therapist?

"We're still working on Rs and Ls," I pointed out.

"You are," Mom agreed, nodding. "But you've made a lot of improvement. Ms. Tink told us about the upcoming book presentations, and we all feel that you should do the speaking part of the presentation next month."

"But-but you always excuse me from speaking."

"Yes, we have in the past," Mom said. "But maybe it's time to try a little harder."

I couldn't believe what they were saying. I did try hard! All the time. Just because my speech had improved didn't mean it was magically easier to speak. Sure, I had spoken to a handful of strangers lately, but a whole class? Twenty-six sets of eyes staring at me?

This was all Ms. Tink's doing. She didn't care about my difficulties.

"Sweet pea, Ms. Tink says you can do so much more than you think," Dad said. "She believes in you."

I doubt that, I thought. *She just can't stand for anyone to not follow her directions.*

I thought then of Elise and the pledge I had made to

her. Pledging wasn't hard when you didn't think you'd have to follow through, but now I knew I'd made a bargain I'd never be able to keep.

The rain didn't let up. Thanksgiving Day came and went. I felt thankful for nothing. All day long, I kept wondering what Birdman was doing. In Chicago. With his little bird.

The day after, I met Orion in the annex. He was looking through the pictures in his *Cosmos* book, the one with the star-spattered cover and all the dog-eared pages.

I interrupted to ask the question I couldn't get off my mind. "How could I get out of a pledge?"

Carefully, he marked his place with a finger and looked up at me. "A pledge?"

"Yes."

"A pledge that you made?"

"Yes."

"To someone else?"

"Yes!" This was getting exasperating.

Orion blinked and frowned. "You can't."

"But I have to!" I wailed. He didn't seem to understand the circumstances. "I only made the pledge because I didn't think I'd have to talk, but now I do, so I can't. I just can't."

Slowly—so slowly—Orion closed his book, placed it in the secret cubby, and shut the door so that it disappeared into the wallpaper.

"No," he said firmly. "If you made a pledge, you have to keep it."

I was about to explain further, but then I saw his hands balled into fists and his eyebrows lowered. Orion was mad—at me. Suddenly I understood. The book, the pledge, Orion's dad—it made sense. Of course Orion didn't want me to break my pledge. He didn't want anyone to feel the sharp edges of a broken promise.

"Right," I said, feeling ashamed that I'd suggested such a thing. It was as if I too had broken a promise to Orion. "I'll keep my pledge."

Orion relaxed but kept glancing at me like he wasn't sure he knew me.

I guessed I'd have to find a way to speak for the presentation. I couldn't let Elise *and* Orion down.

That weekend, while the rain drummed down, I grabbed my secret sketchbook and retreated to the basement, the only place where I could be alone, to work on my creative expression assignment. I settled my back against the freezer, took off my glasses, and squinted at the bare bulb above. The light stretched and feathered, but it did nothing to bite back at the bleakness I felt when I thought about Anne in her annex, working out her dreams on paper but never getting to live them.

I bent my head and drew what I felt, working in a frenzy, leaving no filter between my feelings and the page. I thought about Anne but drew shapes and lines of myself—my frustration at not understanding the simplest things, my hopelessness about speaking.

When I finished, I sat back and smiled. My drawing was not safe. It was not careful. It was bold and frightening—exactly how I wanted it.

Chapter 18

The Monday after Thanksgiving break was soggy but not rainy. I waited for Orion on the sidewalk before school, sending out a breath and hoping to see its white cloud before me. But it wasn't cold enough. As I stood there, I saw someone walking, just rounding the corner from Rock Street onto Amos. I recognized the cane and the limp.

Is Birdman back already? I thought. I ran to the corner, but he was gone.

A wheezy breath came up behind me. "Are you leaving without me?"

I turned and felt a little pang seeing Orion taking an aggravated puff from his inhaler. I hadn't meant to make him run after me. "Sorry," I said, "I just saw . . . someone I thought I knew. Let's go."

It's funny how a secret can grow inside, overtaking the reason for the secret in the first place. At first, I hadn't told

Orion about Birdman because I was mad, then because I wanted Birdman all to myself. Now I didn't have a reason except that I hadn't told him yet.

"I feel like I haven't seen you much lately," Orion said as we walked.

It was a small comment—and he was right—but I felt defensive. I had Birdman and Elise. I couldn't spend all my time with Orion.

"I was just over this weekend," I said.

"Yeah," he said quietly. "I know."

"And besides," I continued, "we can't be each other's only friend."

"Why not?" He stopped and faced me, eyes wide and earnest.

I squirmed under his direct question. Anything true I said might hurt his feelings, so I mumbled, "It's probably not healthy or something," and dropped the subject.

We walked the rest of the way to school in silence. I couldn't tell from Orion's frown if he was mad or deep in thought, but I didn't like feeling bad for wanting other friends. Orion needed to toughen up.

I thought about checking on Orion after school, but I couldn't wait to show my secret sketchbook to Birdman.

Orion would have to wait. I wanted to know why Birdman was back early and why he hadn't told me.

Frouke opened the door and said, "You know he is not here."

"I saw him walking this morning."

Frouke was not embarrassed that I'd caught her in a lie, only put out. "He is resting."

I heard a hammer thumping in the atelier. "Resting?"

She gave an unapologetic shrug and continued to block the doorway.

I'd have to soften her up. "He wants to see me. I know he does." I was his little potato, after all.

The straight line of Frouke's mouth softened. Just a bit.

It was time for phase two. If I could get her to laugh, maybe she would let me through. I took a deep breath.

"Knock-knock."

Frouke's face was blank.

"Knock-knock," I repeated.

Furrowed brow, start of the evil eye.

"You know"—I rapped on the door—"knock-knock."

"Why you knock so many times?" Frouke asked.

I sighed. So much for my plan. "You're supposed to say, 'Who's there?'"

Frouke blinked, her stubby eyelashes taking shallow bows. "I know who is there. You are there."

I shook my head. "It's a joke. I say, 'Knock-knock,' and you say, 'Who's there?'"

"You are there. I have no need of asking."

"It's a knock-knock joke."

Frouke sniffed. "These we do not have in my country."

Hopeless. Nothing kills a joke like explanation, but the firmness of her stance made me determined to see it through.

"Just say, 'Who's there?' OK? Knock-knock."

Frouke rolled her eyes skyward but said, "Who is it?"

Close enough. "Boo."

"Who is this Boo?"

I was getting nowhere. "You're supposed to say, 'Boo who?'"

"You sound like you are crying."

I wilted like a flower in a vase with no water. "That was the joke."

"What?"

"Boo who? You don't have to cry about it. It's only a joke."

Frouke stared at me for a beat, gauging whether I was worth the effort. "Is not funny."

"Well," I mumbled, "you didn't do your part right."

"Americans are not funny. Far better jokes in my country."

I crossed my arms. "Oh yeah? Like what?"

Frouke puffed up her chest. "Why looked the miller out the window?"

"I don't know. Why?" At least I knew the proper response.

"Because he could not see through the door." She looked like she had just handed me a cupcake and wanted to watch me take the first bite.

I smiled. Was that it? "Amusing."

Frouke let out one smileless "Ha!" and turned to lead me down the hallway. "I will take you to him. To spare further . . . jokes."

In the atelier, Birdman was pounding nails willy-nilly into a worn board that looked like it used to be a cupboard door. The nails leaned like stalks of spent corn in a field.

I inched forward. "You're back early."

"Yes," he said, pounding at a nail he'd already bent. "Chicago is not a hospitable city."

I wanted to ask about his little bird, but Birdman's droopy eye looked like it might slide off his face if I pressed him. Instead I said, "I have something to show you—a drawing I've been working on for school."

"So?" he said, setting down the hammer. "Let us have a look."

I flipped to the drawing, my creative expression, as a reel of worries flickered through my head. What if he didn't get it? What if he said it was nothing but shapes and scribbles? What if he called this one safe and careful too?

He held the page at arm's length. For a long time, he said nothing.

"Do you see?" I finally asked.

"Yes, I see. I see the sadness. I see . . . betrayal." He frowned. "But where is the hope?"

I searched my drawing, as if I might suddenly see the hope leap out from behind the charcoal. But I couldn't find it.

Still, he was being unfair. Birdman's paintings weren't about hope. They made me think of wounds and suffering, of being trapped and bound—except the one hanging over his couch.

"Yours don't have hope," I argued. "They're all dark and grim."

He reeled back as if I'd walloped him. "Always there must be hope," he said.

At least he hadn't said my drawing was no good—his was definitely a response from the gut. But I felt a precious, hard-earned thing slipping away, and I didn't know how to pull it back. Birdman was right. There was no hope in my drawing. There was no hope because I didn't feel any when I thought about Anne Frank doomed in her annex. I didn't feel hope about my ability to speak. Maybe someone else could find the hope, but I couldn't.

Suddenly it came to me. "The hope comes from you," I said.

Birdman flinched like I was accusing him.

"From the viewer. You bring the hope." It was so good, I deserved a pat on the back.

"Ah," he said. "Yes. I see." But his droopy eye drifted, and I wondered if he really did.

Birdman frowned down at the board with the nails. Then he handed me a hammer and gave me a thinly brushed smile. "Help me with this. Pull them out. Every one."

Wasn't he just hammering them in? I thought. But he was acting so strangely that I didn't want to question him.

We worked in silence. I pulled nails, and he rummaged in the storage room, bringing out collage after collage, propping them up all over the atelier.

Through my curtain of hair, I watched him survey his paintings. Once, I heard him mutter something about hope. His behavior began to frighten me. Maybe he didn't want me here. Maybe all those times Frouke sent me away had been because he could only tolerate me one day a week. But I was paying off a debt. I couldn't stop until that was done.

The next time Birdman came out of the storage room, I asked, "How long before I've worked off my debt?"

"What?"

"For breaking the glass ball. When will I have paid you back for that?"

He looked up, sharply. "Why do you ask such a question?"

I couldn't voice what I feared. "I just wanted to know."

"You are anxious to leave? You feel bound to me? Go then! Go back to drawing your little ponies. I don't need you. Your debt is paid."

My cheeks burned, and my throat squeezed tight. All I could get out was, "No . . . I . . ."

"Frouke is right. This is not a good thing." He clomped into the storage room, his knee buckling with each step.

I stood there like an idiot, as if my feet had been nailed down. What had I said? What had I done?

"We are finished." Birdman came out carrying a blue-green collage I loved. Without making eye contact, he said, "I have work to do."

Silently I watched him bang open an easel and set up

for painting. Tears swarmed to my eyes, but I held them back. I felt like the glass ball—cracked open and empty inside.

I stood there while he brought out paints. I stood there while he brought out brushes. I stood there while he brought out a palette. I knew that if he looked at me, he would see everything—that I didn't care about the debt, that I would come and work with him as long as he would let me, that I was sorry for whatever I had done to ruin everything.

But he didn't look at me. The longer he ignored me, the smaller I felt. His ignoring filled the room and pressed me on all sides, until I felt compacted like a junk car. My nose stung from holding back the tears. If I stayed any longer I would bawl like a baby, so I turned, walked out, and closed the door behind me.

Outside, I ran—around the house and down the driveway—tears splashing my lenses. When I stopped for breath, I found my hand still clutched the hammer. I stared at it stupidly. I could drop it and keep running. I could stuff it in the mailbox. I could keep it and use it as a reason to come back later. But those would be the easy things.

I sniffed the snot back into my nose, wiped the tears with my sleeve, and headed back to the atelier. I would return the hammer. I would tell Birdman I didn't care about the debt. We would laugh at the misunderstanding.

I approached from the outside door and saw him through the windows. He slumped in front of a painting I loved. Driftwood teemed at the bottom. Above, a calm expanse of blue-green. It reminded me of river and sky.

The weight of the hammer pulled at my arm. I should have walked away, but I couldn't drag my eyes from his hunched shoulders.

Then Birdman stirred. He took up a brush, tapped it in a daub of paint, and made a black V-slash in the sky of the painting.

A whimper escaped my lips.

Slash after slash after slash. An angry flock of birds blotting out the sky. Each slash stabbed at my heart. I loved that painting, and he was ruining it.

Finally he dipped a wide brush into the can of black paint and swept a thick line across the river. Another dip. Black over the birds, over the blue-green. He blotted out the river. He blotted out the sky.

When the painting was completely black, Birdman dropped his head into his hands and began to shake, still holding the wide paintbrush. One thick black glob dripped from the bristles onto his head. Right onto the shiny bald spot.

I stepped backward. Something was deeply, horribly wrong, and somehow, I was the cause of it all. What had I done to make him destroy his painting?

I saw my secret sketchbook lying on the table, still open to my hopeless drawing. There wasn't a muscle in me strong enough to enter the atelier to retrieve it. Forget every hard thing. This was too hard.

It was then that Birdman looked up. At me, I thought, but maybe there was too much glare. I saw in his eyes a pool of regret that stretched past me, out to whatever horizon he searched for. It was a wild look. I stumbled back, turned, and ran.

The hammer was still in my hand, so I circled to the front of the house and placed it on the doorstep. As I turned away, the front door swung open. Frouke filled the doorway, frowning with every part of her body.

"Why you upset him?" she demanded "You are supposed to make him happy. Help him. Why you bring up the past?"

"I-I didn't," I stammered. "I only asked—"

"You only, you only! You only a girl. You never think. Don't you know he is sick?" She picked up the hammer and pointed it at me. "You go." She slammed the door.

I stood motionless, stunned by the unfairness of it all. No, I didn't know he was sick. He hadn't looked sick to me.

And what kind of sick was she talking about? Sick with a cold? Or really sick? Hospital-sick? Dying-sick?

I crunched down the gravel drive. Wet fir branches hung low, lobbing heavy drops down on my head, neck, and shoulders. Birdman's words—"We are finished"—ricocheted in my head. I wished that I too could black out that moment with paint and brush.

Chapter 19

That week I didn't draw. I didn't sketch. Every time I reached for a pencil, every time I found myself doodling, I thought of Birdman—the black slashes on his blue-green collage, the glob of paint on his bald spot, the pool of regret in his eyes—and dropped my pencil as if it had burned me.

At home Benny was teething and crying too much for Mom and Dad to notice anything wrong with me. Only Jordyn did.

"Hey, space monkey," she said when she caught me staring at the ceiling in our room. "Come back to PE."

I blinked. PE. Planet Earth.

"BT, huh?"

"What?"

"Boy Troubles."

"Not everything is about boys."

Jordyn shrugged. "If you say so." She shook her head in pity.

Orion noticed too. But instead of comfort, I got an argument.

"Something on your mind?" he asked when I walked into the annex.

The complicated knot he handed me said he had something on *his* mind. He always gave me difficult knots when he was irritated.

I stayed silent. I couldn't tell him what had happened without starting at the beginning. And then I'd have to explain why I hadn't told him about Birdman earlier. That would make him more irritated.

So instead I stared at the knot. It wasn't like his trick one that came undone with two sharp tugs. This one seemed impossible to untangle.

"You know, you don't have to hang out with me if you don't want to," he finally said.

I was floored. Was everyone going crazy?

"Of course I want to hang out with you! I just don't want to hang out with *only* you!"

Orion nodded, and we left it at that, but I suspected this knot would get more tangled before it came loose.

On Thursday, I mustered my courage and marched to the end of Rock Street. I would use my left-behind sketchbook as an excuse to see if Birdman had meant what he'd said about us being finished.

Probably he will apologize, I told myself as I walked. Probably he would explain that he wasn't himself. The trip to Chicago had been a strain. He would ruffle my hair, call me his little potato, and together we would paint over the black.

But standing in front of the empty pedestal, my pep talk sounded hollow. Something had happened in Chicago, something with his little bird, and I had made it worse.

If this was a glimpse of the tortured-artist life, I didn't want it. Some hard things were too hard.

I turned and went home.

Elise showed concern in her own aloof way. We'd finished reading Anne Frank's diary and were supposed to be working on our presentations, which would start next month. But in class on Friday, she said, "What does it mean, I wonder, when the girl who draws suddenly stops drawing?"

"It means I have nothing to draw."

"No inspiration?"

"Something like that," I said.

Elise squinted, as if trying to feather the light inside me. "Sometimes we artists have to just keep on creating. Sometimes it's the only way."

Ms. Tink wove in and out of the desk islands. Most groups were already deep into their scripts and visual aids. Elise and I hadn't even decided on a theme.

"You'll still be able to speak in front of everyone, right?" Elise looked worried.

"Um . . ." My throat began to squeeze. I hadn't told her about the parent-teacher conference. As far as she knew, nothing had changed.

"You've spoken in front of the class before, right?"

I shook my head.

"What about last year?" Elise asked.

Another head shake.

"The year before?"

I looked down.

"Have you *ever* spoken in front of the class? Like maybe in kindergarten?"

I thought back to circle time. The big plush carpet with colored squares for us to sit on. I remembered Ms. Holly's patient smile and kind voice. I remembered working on our letter sounds—lots of *mmmmming* and *t-t-t-t-ing* that felt like buzzing in my ears.

But what I remembered most was the panic of not knowing what was happening when it was my turn to answer. What had the question been? What did Ms. Holly want me to say? I never knew. All the other kids seemed to, but there was a lag between when someone spoke and when I understood. How did the other kids figure it out so fast?

"I don't think my kindergarten teacher ever heard the sound of my voice," I told Elise.

In English, we read a poem written by a woman—Emily Dickinson—who hardly ever left her own house. Usually, I didn't *get* poems, but this one spoke in a voice I understood.

"Hope" is the thing with feathers—
That perches in the soul—
And sings the tune without the words—
And never stops—at all—

And sweetest—in the Gale—is heard—
And sore must be the storm—
That could abash the little Bird
That kept so many warm—

I've heard it in the chillest land—
And on the strangest Sea—
Yet, never, in Extremity,
It asked a crumb—Of Me.

We were supposed to write about what the author was trying to say about hope, but I wasn't thinking in words. My pencil sketched a little bird perched inside Birdman. But when I tried to make the bird sing, it looked like it was hungry instead. I thought of my sketchbook, sprawled open on Birdman's work table, open to my hopeless drawing.

I couldn't leave him with no hope.

I re-read the poem. At the end, it seemed to say I didn't have to do anything for the bird to keep singing. But I didn't trust that was true. Not for Birdman.

Maybe Elise was right—I had to keep creating. *That's* what the hope-bird asked of me. I might not have the courage to go see Birdman, but I could at least draw for him. I would start the next day.

Chapter 20

At the bottom of Orion's backyard, where trim lawn gave way to the tall yellow grass of the oak grove, there was a stump. I spread my raincoat over it and sat facing the swooping tree.

The swooping tree was the oldest oak in the grove. Mrs. Em had told me once that it was at least four hundred years old. The wide trunk divided into swollen limbs that split again and again on their way up. Ferns sprouted from crooks of branches. Moss clung to one side.

And then there was that swooping branch. It started high, swooped low until it almost touched the ground, then rose back up again. That branch was not giving up. Neither was the tree.

That's why I chose to draw it.

I began with vine charcoal, laying down the shape of the trunk. For the branches, I switched to a 2B pencil—softer than a school pencil, but not so soft that everything smeared. I tried to look at the tree more than the paper, to let my eyes follow the branches and trust my hand to keep up. But my eyes kept losing track of the twists and turns.

Ugh! I thought, looking down at my first attempt. *A preschooler could scribble something better.* I didn't feel like I was *seeing* anything. I'd never be able to do fifty drawings. Or even twenty. Or two.

A raindrop splatted down onto my paper, then another and another. Quickly I packed up, dashed through the kitchen door of the Emerson house, and stood dripping on the rug. Orion hadn't been home when I arrived—I'd stopped by the annex to say hello—and I still didn't see him now.

Mrs. Em, however, waltzed by and glanced at my still-open sketchbook. "Nice octopus."

I sighed. "It's supposed to be a tree."

"Oops," she said, coming around to look right-side-up. "I see. Yes. There it is. The raindrops looked like sea urchins."

At least she was honest. I flipped the sketchbook closed. It would be a long time before I had something to show Birdman.

It was still raining the next day when I popped into the annex. Orion paused the instructional video he was watching on his tablet and let out a frustrated groan. Robotics pieces littered the floor around him, and his rover looked like a belly-up spider.

"What's wrong?" I hoped I hadn't caused the frustration.

"I don't have the right piece, and I'm trying to substitute other pieces, and it's just not working."

Things had been normal between us on our walks to school, but our argument still felt fresh. I wanted to smooth it over with something good and pure.

"Wanna rig up something else?" I grinned wide.

"What do you have in mind?"

"I'm drawing our tree, and I need a rain shelter."

Orion's face lit up with a big, goofy smile like I'd thrown him a surprise birthday party. He loved a technical challenge.

Minutes later, he had strung up a blue tarp between two trees and set a lawn chair beneath it. His breath came out in wheezes.

"Perfect," I said, sitting and opening my sketchbook.

"What are you drawing this for, anyway?" he asked.

My stomach knotted. There was no reason not to tell him. "It's an assignment."

"From school?" He took a puff from his inhaler.

I was going to tell him everything. Really, I was. But something else came out of my mouth. "It's more of a personal project. I'm doing one hundred drawings of the same tree."

Orion let out a low whistle. "Why?"

"Why what?"

"Why are you doing so many drawings of one tree?"

"To understand it." It was the truth, but it felt like a lie because of what I left out.

Orion nodded and then frowned at his handiwork. "It'll do for now. But you'll have to lift the middle when it fills with rain." He demonstrated with a rake, pressing the tines up against the tarp until water gushed over the edges. "You're going to want something portable, so you can draw from different angles."

"You're right. I hadn't thought of that."

Orion grinned. "That's what you have me for."

I saw an idea lighting up behind his eyes before he dashed back to the house. He ran through the rain without even putting up his hood.

My drawing started OK, with the trunk splitting into five thick limbs, but after that it became a tangled mess. There were too many branches. How would I ever draw them all? I did four drawings, each one worse than the previous, before giving up. The last one looked like a map of the circulatory system drawn by a blind person.

In the annex, I taped up my drawings from today, plus yesterday's octopus, to examine them. Orion was busy with the notepad he kept for knots and inventions. The rover kit was gone, replaced by lengths of white PVC pipe, a ratchet cutter, and a jar of glue.

"What are you making?" I asked.

He hunched over the notepad to hide his sketch. "You'll see."

I turned back to my drawings and groaned. "Why can't I draw this stupid tree?"

"They look nice," Orion said.

"Art isn't about nice." Birdman's words left a bitter trail in my mouth. "It's about making you feel something."

Orion cocked his head to the side, as if listening to a voice he hadn't heard before. "Do you have to draw the whole thing at once? Maybe you should try to understand one part at a time."

I stared at him. One part at a time. Of course. Orion was brilliant! I wanted to throw my arms around him and squeeze, but instead I threw a pillow at his head. I missed by a mile.

The next time I came to draw the stupid tree, Orion had a surprise for me.

"Don't go outside yet," he said. "Come with me. I'm almost finished."

"Finished with what?"

"You'll see!"

Orion danced around like a kid before Christmas. His excitement was contagious. I knew he wouldn't reveal his surprise until he was ready, so I followed him to the garage. He waded through the jungle of stuff, stooping to gather what he needed—duct tape, large scissors, and twine. Then he moved on to a drawer full of nuts and bolts and screws and hooks.

"I need all the eyelets," he said, and together we hunted down every last shiny metal ring.

It reminded me, briefly, of the drawers in Birdman's atelier, only his were organized. I felt a little ache, like a pinch of tender skin, thinking of Birdman.

Orion made me close my eyes as he led me down the back stairs and across the soggy yard. When we reached the grass, he said, "Ta-da!"

I opened my eyes to see a lawn-chair throne with PVC pipe forming a sort of canopy frame over the top. Three sides were protected by blue tarp.

"I just need to attach the top." Orion unfurled the last

piece of tarp, cut it to size, attached a few eyelets along each edge, and threaded lengths of twine through the holes. Then he threw the canopy piece over the frame and tied it in place.

I couldn't stop smiling. This was Orion at his finest. He might not be the coolest guy out there—or the strongest or cutest—but the way he put things together was amazing. He invented new purposes, fresh uses for everything. A cracked wheelbarrow could be an herb garden for Mrs. Em. A set of old keys could be bent into little wall hooks. Orion saw things differently than other people. Maybe he saw the essence of things. Maybe that was more important than suffering.

"What do you think?" Orion's feet squelched on the soggy ground.

I was still staring at this creation he made just for me. "Orion," I said, "you are an artist."

Over the next week, the rain came down, but I stayed dry. Orion had made my drawing throne light, so I shifted around the tree, trying to see from different angles. I thought I could redraw what had gone wrong between Birdman and me. My drawings were like snapshots of my feelings.

#6: I drew a round clump of mistletoe high in the branches, feathery like hope.

#7: I drew gnarled roots.

#8: I drew deep and angry ruts in the bark. Birdman shouldn't have destroyed his painting. He could have blacked out something ugly—something nobody wanted.

#9: I drew the knobs on the trunk, evidence of some injury, perhaps a century ago. Suddenly it occurred to me that maybe Birdman's anger had nothing to do with what I'd done. Maybe he had injuries from the past. Maybe he would have blacked out his painting anyway.

That day—a Thursday—I almost went to see him. But I thought of my secret sketchbook splayed on his work table and remembered his question: *Where is the hope?*

I couldn't go see him until I had hope to bring.

So I drew the tree—#10—and drew the tree—#11—and drew—#12.

#13: I drew the spot where the trunk divided. Five branches grew away from each other, splitting and becoming smaller. I drew from the center out. The center was the strength. Hope fluttered around the edges.

The more I thought about hope, the more certain I became that the poem we'd read in English was wrong. The little hope-bird didn't belong inside. It belonged out so it could fly from branch to branch, perch on one shoulder and the next.

With every stroke of the pencil, I sent a little hope-bird from me to Birdman.

#14: I took off my glasses and squinted up at the pieces of sky between branches. The white light burst through and feathered, and everywhere there were wings of light shining through the branches.

As I drew, a knot came loose inside me, and sketch by sketch, I forgave Birdman.

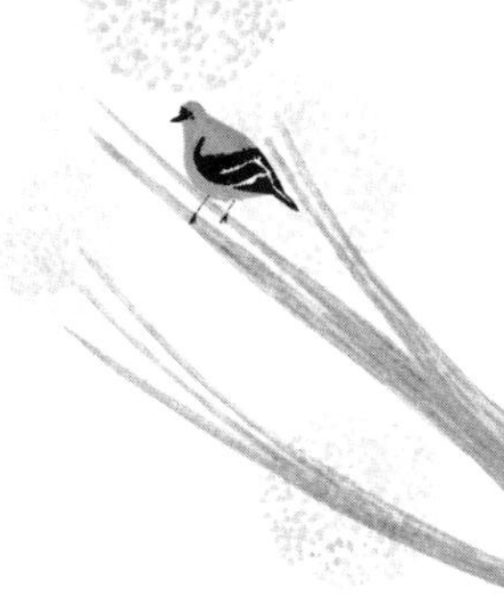

Chapter 21

The weekend before our presentation was due, Elise and I still didn't have anything to show. We planned a sleepover to work it out. We were both stressed about finishing on time, but while I dragged my feet, Elise was all business.

"All we have to do," she said as we walked to her house Friday after school, "is find a topic, write a script, and memorize it."

"And create visual aids," I said. "We need those too."

"You can throw those together easy."

I smiled, but I could feel the fakeness in my cheeks. I was still hoping for a miracle to swoop in and save me at the last minute. I couldn't picture myself speaking in front of the class. I couldn't do it.

At Elise's house, I took every opportunity to avoid getting started. We got a snack—crackers and peanut butter.

Then drinks—chocolate milk. Then we watched a couple of epic fail videos to take a break before starting.

When Elise suggested acting out a scene from Anne's diary, I said, "Yeah, maybe," and offered to help Evan make a pillow cave for his dinosaurs on the living room floor.

"All right," Elise sighed and joined us. "But after this we get to work."

"Sure," I said, knowing she was right but not wanting to move us any closer to that moment when I would have to speak.

It was dark out by the time Elise's mom came home hefting a thick stack of papers. And Elise and I still didn't have anything to present.

"Hey, kiddos," Charla said. "I have to go through these documents tonight. Mind if we do a popcorn dinner?"

"Yay!" Evan shouted. He made his T-rex and triceratops high-five.

Elise's mouth went to the side. "Can we make any kind we want?"

"Sky's the limit," said her mom.

"OK, but you owe me a lasagna dinner."

"You got it."

"With garlic bread—no salad."

"Salad for me, and it's a deal."

They shook hands.

Charla parked herself on the couch and slipped in earbuds while we went off to the kitchen. We popped three giant bowls of popcorn and topped them with combinations of butter, sugar, salt, cheddar-cheese seasoning, and chocolate chips.

This would never happen at my house. My mom was busy, but she liked to oversee everything to make sure it was done properly. Dinner always included vegetables.

"It's cool that you get to eat whatever you want," I whispered, glancing at Charla, who was watching the news on her tablet while flipping through the documents and taking notes.

As we munched, we watched videos of pets making unwise leaps and doing hilarious and painful-looking acrobatics.

"Some of these are so staged," Elise said. A moment later she sprang up. "That's it!"

"What?"

"I know how we'll get you to speak for the presentation."

"How?" I asked, cringing. I needed more time to psych myself up.

"We'll make a video ahead of time," Elise told me. "That way you won't have to get up in front of the entire class—just the camera."

I imagined myself speaking into the eye of a lens, and

my throat tightened. At least it was only one eye, compared to twenty-six sets of eyes. But still. I swallowed and croaked out the only delaying tactic I could think of: "What are we going to film? We still don't have a script."

Elise sat back on her heels. "You're right." Then her eyes lit on her mom's screen, and a slow smile spread across her face.

"What?" I asked.

"We're going to do a newscast!" said Elise, triumphantly. "You'll be a reporter." She grabbed a stray brachiosaurus and held it like a microphone. "This is Clarity Kartoffel reporting live from the pages of history."

My heart sank. Elise had locked onto the idea. There was no way to put it off any longer.

We retreated to the kitchen table with the bowl of popcorn to write our script. As I picked chocolaty pieces out of the bowl and doodled in the margins, Elise was busy on her phone.

"All set," she said finally. "We'll film tomorrow. I got us a camera and tripod."

"Can't we just use your phone?" I asked, alarmed. A real camera seemed so formal.

"This'll be way more professional," she said. "Besides, Orion's stepdad has all the stuff. He's an amateur photographer."

I felt knocked off-balance. An avalanche of thoughts crashed down on me. I knew that Javier dabbled in photography, but how did Elise know? How did she know Orion at all? He was in a different class. I'd never seen them talking on the playground or at lunch.

"You were texting Javier?" I asked, confused.

"No, Orion."

"How do you know Orion?"

Elise gave me her hard-as-glass look. "You're not the only one who can have friends, you know."

"It's not that. I didn't mean—"

"And you're not his only friend."

"It's not that either! It's just . . ." I couldn't finish. I didn't know why I felt this burning inside, as if I'd swallowed something too hot too quickly. Of course they could both have other friends. It was just that. . . .

"I didn't know you even knew each other," I finished lamely.

"Yeah, well, we do." Elise tipped her face away from me, like I wasn't on the inside anymore. "Anyway, I was talking to Orion the other day—"

"Where?" I interrupted. I didn't understand why neither of them had said anything. Then again, maybe I'd missed the cues. It wouldn't have been the first time.

"What does it matter where?"

"It doesn't," I said. But I couldn't leave it alone. "I just don't understand when you became friends."

Elise turned on me, impatient. "We see each other at recess, and we're in robotics club together. He's really good at programming."

"Yeah, I know." I was annoyed to hear something I already knew. "He's *my* best friend."

"No need to get snippy. I was only answering your question." She turned back to our script. "Now, can we write this thing?"

"Of course," I said, remembering my pledge.

But as we wrote the script and practiced our lines, my brain kept spinning with thoughts of the friends Orion might have—friends I knew nothing about—and the chocolate popcorn left a bitter smear on my tongue.

Chapter 22

Elise feathered the makeup brush over my eyelids, and I imagined myself as someone else, someone who wouldn't shrink from a camera lens, someone who was fine with her best friend making new friends. Perfectly fine with it.

But then I thought about that surprised look on Orion's face when I'd said we should have other friends. Had he already made friends with Elise then? But then why wouldn't he have said so?

Elise had been drilling me on my lines all morning, but she'd fallen silent while doing my makeup. "Voilà!" she finally said, turning me to the mirror.

I saw a strange blur.

"Oops," Elise said, "forgot the glasses." She slipped them over my ears.

I gasped. My hair fell in glossy waves. The makeup

and work suit we had borrowed from Charla made me look like an adult. I was not Clarity Kartoffel. I was Monique Silverthorn.

From Elise's house, we walked to Rock Street. At first I felt self-conscious, not wanting anyone to see me, but as we trudged up the hill, I began to feel the freedom of being someone else. By the time we turned onto Rock Street, I was swinging my hips and tossing my hair for anyone who cared to see.

Orion was waiting for us on his front porch. When he saw me, he stared. One corner of his mouth turned up. "Whoa. You look . . . different."

"That," said Elise, "is the whole point."

Orion kept glancing at me sideways, and his breath came out raspy.

"Don't have an asthma attack." I tried to sound nonchalant, but I felt shy again with him looking at me that way.

Elise bumped her shoulder against Orion's, and they talked and laughed like this was so much fun. I turned away, toward the bird tree. The morning was full of finches, all crammed together. I wanted to fly there and be silent among the chattering birds.

"Javier says we can use his equipment," Orion said, "but I have to be the one operating the camera."

"Fine with me," said Elise. "I'm directing."

Orion went inside to get the camera and tripod. I hadn't pictured him being a part of this. He thought I was brave. I didn't want him to see me fail so miserably.

"I thought you were filming," I said to Elise.

"I can't film *and* direct," she said. "What's the problem?"

"Nothing, it's just that . . ." I felt bombarded on all sides. I was angry at Elise for making me do this. Angry at Orion for looking at me in that dopey way. "I didn't know."

"You like him, don't you?" Elise asked.

"Like who?"

"You know who. Orion."

A short, sharp laugh escaped my mouth—meaner than I'd intended. "We've been friends since we were babies."

"He's a cool guy."

"Yeah," I said. *I* thought he was amazing, but I was pretty sure other people thought he was weird.

"Kinda cute."

"I guess." I didn't think about Orion in that way.

Suddenly I felt sick. Did Elise like Orion? Standing there in makeup, I felt like a kid playing dress up. It was a dumb idea to do every hard thing. It was a dumb idea to be a real artist.

"I can't do this."

Elise looked me in the eye. "Of course you can. We'll help you."

But I felt beyond help.

Down at the creek, Elise repositioned me in front of the old mill yet again. We'd been at it all morning.

"OK, Clarity," she said. "You are a glamorous reporter and you are standing at the ruins of a building that has just been bombed. You are about to report on wartime atrocities. You can do this." She backed away, keeping eye contact.

I nodded. I knew my lines, but the camera lens kept sucking me down to a hopeless place. I couldn't gulp enough air or courage to get them out.

"And, action!" Elise called.

Orion pressed the button, the green light came on, and I stared into the dark lens. Beside me, I heard the creek rushing past. I gathered my breath, but it was no use. For the millionth time, my throat tightened, my tongue thickened, and I choked.

"Cut!" Elise shouted.

Orion came out from behind the camera and puffed out his cheeks. He was tired of this too.

"This isn't working," Elise said.

"That's because I can't do it," I said.

"Yes, you can." She had been patient with me so far. "Stop saying that. Quit being a baby."

"Um, guys," said Orion. "The camera says low battery. We need to get this in the next try."

My stomach twisted, and my voice burrowed even deeper under the added pressure.

"Darn it, Clarity, you said you could do this!" Elise threw down her clipboard and stomped off along the bank, ripping up tall grasses as she went and throwing them into the creek.

Orion came up next to me. I watched the water slip by. Being friends with Orion was easy compared to Elise. He forgave me when I messed up. But Elise demanded hard things.

"Clara," Orion said, "if you don't want to do this . . ."

Suddenly a surge of determination rose in me. Orion was handing me an out, but I wouldn't take it. No more burrowing. Elise had shown me her dream wall. She had let me inside. And I had made her a promise—a pledge. I had to let her in, mushy words and all.

"OK!" I called to her. "I'm ready."

Elise turned halfway. "Only if you're actually going to do it, Clarity."

I straightened my shoulders and tossed my hair. "I'm not Clarity. Call me Monique Silverthorn."

Elise regarded me for a moment, then picked up her clipboard. "OK, Monique. Let's see what you've got."

"Woo-hoo!" said Orion.

Elise leveled her gaze at him. "This isn't a sporting event. Get the camera ready."

I took my place.

"And, action."

The green light came on. Like every time, my throat squeezed tight. I was failing again—I could feel it. As if sensing my panic, Orion pulled his face out from behind the camera and smiled his dopey smile. Just for me.

Elise leaned in. "C'mon, Monique."

I looked at both of their bright faces. They believed I could do it, even though I'd failed a million times already. They were bringing the hope.

In that moment I was so grateful for my friends. I opened my mouth and—wonder of wonders—words came out. Clear, sparkling words. "This is Monique Silverthorn, reporting to you live from a site of terrible destruction."

But I didn't need Monique Silverthorn. There was a Clarity inside me that spoke directly to Orion and Elise.

When it was over, when I'd said all the words, Elise

let loose her tinkling laugh and threw her arms around me. "You did it! I knew you could do it! Didn't I tell you?"

I was breathless as she spun me around. I had climbed a mountain. Run a marathon.

"We knew you could do it all along," Elise said, turning to Orion, "didn't we?"

Orion put his hands in his pockets. "Yup," he said.

Behind the two of them, the sun was setting, rays slanting through the trees and shining like stars. I squinted, and the light feathered out like wings. Wings behind Orion. Wings behind Elise. Wings in the sky all around.

There was still the actual presentation to get through on Tuesday. But the hardest part was over—or so I thought.

Chapter 23

After the triumph of speaking in front of a camera, I felt so light and free that I drew wings on everything. I turned every doodle and sketch into a hope-bird until I couldn't stand it any longer. I had to share this feeling. Tomorrow Elise and I would give our presentation, but today I headed down Rock Street to bring the hope.

It had been nearly three weeks since I'd last visited Birdman. I might not understand my tree, even after twenty-three drawings, but I could show him these new hope-sketches.

My breath formed icy clouds, and there was a crackle in the air as I passed the empty pedestal. Frouke opened and filled the doorway when I knocked. She wore the smug expression of a supervillain who knew the superhero would come eventually.

Oh. I'd forgotten that I'd have to get past her.

"So," she said, "you come back."

I tried to summon the Clarity that Orion and Elise had drawn out of me. "I've got something to show him."

"Mr. Vogelman is not available." She spoke formally, as if she didn't know me.

"But I need to see him."

"He does not need to see you. Always you bring pain." Frouke narrowed her eyes to slits. If she *had* been a supervillain, laser beams would have shot out. "He needs to rest. You go."

Frouke began to turn away but I stopped her with my words. "You said he was sick. Is he still sick?"

She didn't answer, only sighed. Her silence confirmed my suspicions. Birdman had more than a cold.

Then I remembered my plan. If I could make Frouke laugh, maybe she would let me in or at least answer my questions. If Frouke could laugh, anything was possible.

"Knock-knock," I said.

Frouke placed her fists on her hips. "I know you already."

"Just say, 'Who's there?'"

Frouke's lips tightened to the thinnest possible line. Then, in a high, fake-sounding voice, she said, "Who is it that is knocking at my door?"

"Police."

"Why are the police at my door?"

I got the feeling she was being dim on purpose, but I plunged forward. "Police may I come in?"

Frouke didn't laugh. She didn't even smile. She did the opposite. Her mouth turned down at the corners. "Is not funny," she declared and closed the door.

That crackle was still in the air as I walked home. A shimmering halo surrounded each streetlight. The slightest squint feathered the light and turned it into wings.

Frouke had said I brought pain. But she was wrong. I was bringing the hope. I knew Birdman wanted to see me. He had to. I was his little potato.

I wouldn't let Frouke stand in my way. Every day I would knock on his door. Every day I would bring the hope until Frouke let me in.

It started snowing that night—big, fat, steady flakes—and continued through morning, giving us two snow days right before Christmas break. My miracle had happened after all.

I used Mom's phone to text Elise:

Guess we get out of the presentation!!!!

We'll have to make it up after break.

That's next year. Why worry, just enjoy!!!!

That morning, Elise and I met up with Orion and a bunch of neighborhood kids for sledding and snowball fights. Even with all that activity, Orion only needed his inhaler twice. We played like little kids, and I didn't worry who was friends with who. The snow lightened everything.

That afternoon, I knocked on Birdman's door. When Frouke opened it, I skipped the pleasantries.

"Why can't I see him?"

"He is not available," Frouke said.

"How sick is he?"

"His health I do not discuss."

"What happened in Chicago?"

"It is not for me to say."

"Why did he come back early?"

"That is no business of yours."

These questions were going nowhere. Time to change tactics.

"I need my sketchbook back."

"Pah," she huffed. "Nothing of yours is here."

"Yes, it is. I left my sketchbook in the atelier."

Frouke sniffed but said, "I look for it." She didn't move.

"Now?" I prompted.

"Not now." She folded her arms beneath her bosom.

I wasn't giving up. "Knock-knock."

Frouke said nothing.

"Knock-knock."

"Who is there?" she relented.

"Banana."

"What banana?"

"Knock-knock."

"Who is there again?"

"Banana."

"Who banana?"

"Knock-knock."

"This game I will not play."

"Knock-knock."

Silence.

"Knock-knock."

Silent as a rock.

"Knock-knock."

"Ach, mijn hemel."

I didn't stop to figure out what that meant. "Knock-knock."

"Who is there?"

"Orange."

"Orange who?"

"Orange you glad I didn't say banana again?"

Without even the twitch of a smile, Frouke said, "No. I am glad you didn't say 'knock-knock' again. I am becoming sleepy of all the knocking. Better joke from my country." She cleared her throat. "What is yellow and teases?"

"I don't know. What?"

"Banana-na-na-NA-na." She shut the door.

That was actually funny, but I refused to laugh. Evil woman and her evil jokes.

I would have to get sneaky.

I crept around the side of the house to the atelier. My shoes crunched through the snow, and I laid my nose against the cold glass, fogging it with my breath. It was dark inside. No hint of activity. Everything looked undisturbed and neatly put away. My secret sketchbook no longer lay on the worktable. Where was it?

I tried the doorknob, but it was locked. Great! How could I bring the hope if Frouke wouldn't let me?

I turned to leave, feeling frustrated, when I saw the pure white blanket of snow covering the lawn outside the atelier. No kids had tromped through it. No one had rolled a snowball trail to reveal the mud and grass beneath.

It was a perfect canvas.

Taking large, careful steps, I walked to the center, faced the house, and fell backward, flat onto my back. I swept my arms up and down as I moved my legs in and out. When I was done, I tiptoed away. Now when Birdman looked outside, he would see the hope I had left for him.

Chapter 24

The snow melted quickly, and I went back to drawing my tree. Elise was visiting her grandparents in California over Christmas, so I wouldn't see her until after the break—a good excuse not to think about the presentation at all.

I was in Orion's yard, drawing pieces of sky showing through branches—#26—when I rolled my pencil off its tip, using the side to make rough, expressive lines. I'd never seen the tree like this before. I was on the brink of a breakthrough. I could feel it.

Suddenly I heard Orion's wheezy breath beside me. A piece of paper crinkled in his hand. I didn't know how long he'd been standing there, but I couldn't stop to talk. Like magic, the branches took shape on their own. I drew in a rush, trying to get it all down before the light changed.

Orion said something, but I only heard murmurs. His

presence was like someone trying to pull me from a dream. I could feel it slipping away. I hung on and kept drawing.

Finally Orion cleared his throat like he wanted a response.

"What?" I said, not lifting my eyes from the paper.

"I'm trying to tell you about the letter," he said. "From my dad."

All at once, I realized what I was doing. I was seeing the tree's essence. Like Birdman had taught me to do with the horses. Like seeing Elise in her dream wall.

Now I understood why I had to do so many drawings. It took work to find essence. Work to see it. Work to hang on to it. Work to channel it through the pencil and onto the page. It took time—like making a friend took time.

I glanced at Orion. He held perfectly still, mouth tense, still waiting for a response.

"Right," I said. "Your dad?" I flipped to a new page, laying down light, energetic swaths. Now that I knew what I was doing, I couldn't wait to draw more. "It's not your birthday. Why did he write? Is he OK?"

"He's fine."

I added detail, rolling the shadow around the trunk and leaving light to reveal the pattern of bark. Orion often took long pauses to collect his thoughts, so I didn't worry when he said nothing. I just kept drawing. The uppermost branches strained for the top of the page but didn't quite make it. Above them was two inches of sky. I liked the effect. The tree could be reaching for anything. Maybe I would hang this drawing in the secret annex.

I turned to show Orion.

He wasn't there.

Chapter 25

My snow angel had melted days ago, but still, Frouke wouldn't let me in. I could only hope Birdman had seen it. Each day I came up with a new joke.

"Knock-knock."

"Who is it?"

"Sherwood."

"Who is Sherwood?"

"Sherwood like to come in."

Each time, Frouke countered with her own joke.

"Why does the witch fly on a broomstick?"

"I don't know. Why?"

"Because the vacuum cleaner is too heavy."

And each time, she shut the door.

When I wasn't knocking on Birdman's door, I was

drawing, heading straight for Orion's backyard without stopping in the annex. With each sketch, I found more ways to capture the tree's essence. Fun ways. I drew with crayons, colored pencils, and the oil pastels I'd gotten from Aunt Lindy. I even tried finger paints, but my fingers froze in minutes. I drew my tree in scribbles—circles and jagged lines. I darkened the negative space between branches, leaving the tree itself clear and white.

I loved the thought that Orion and I were both working on our separate things—me drawing, him on his Mars rover. I kept him in the balloon-bubble of my mind, looking forward to that moment when we would share what we'd accomplished.

After one more drawing, I kept thinking.

By Christmas Eve, I was up to thirty-three drawings, and I still hadn't seen Orion. At home, we had a big ham dinner with a tablecloth, napkin rings, and sparkling cider. Afterwards, Mom and Dad drank coffee in the kitchen. I was about to slip out to knock on Birdman's door when I heard their voices drop low.

A secret at Christmastime was too delicious to resist, so I pressed up against the hallway wall to listen. I was only able to catch snatches of the conversation.

". . . in the hospital . . ."

". . . she doesn't know . . ."

". . . over there every day . . ."

I barely heard the rest. Panic squeezed my windpipe, and I thought immediately of Orion. My mind flashed back to that time at the creek, when his lips had turned blue and he'd been unable to breathe. If he'd had a bad attack, one bad enough to land him in the hospital, I had to go to him.

Dad's voice cut through my panic: "Ever tried getting a straight answer out of that woman? She's like a rock."

A slow dawn broke in me. I knew a woman who was like a rock. She guarded Birdman's doorway. Dad was talking about Birdman, not Orion.

My breathing evened out, but a new panic rose—not sharp and wild but slow and roiling, like the tide going out and taking something precious with it. Birdman was sick. I knew that. Frouke had said as much. But if what my parents said was true, Birdman was in the hospital. Frouke had made it seem like he was right there in the house.

Time to find out what was going on.

Frouke flung open the door. She wore an apron with tiny Christmas trees embroidered on it. Before I could open my mouth, she said, "A man came to the doctor with a tulip growing out from his ear."

"Huh?"

"A tulip," she yelled, as if I was hard of hearing, "growing out from his ear."

Oh, I realized. *A joke*.

"The doctor, he says, 'That is very strange,'" she continued. "'I know,' says the man. 'I sowed radishes.'"

I was still getting the joke, which was kind of funny, when Frouke held out a folded piece of paper. I stared at it stupidly. "What is it?" I asked.

"He write you something."

My heart quickened as I snatched the paper from her. I hoped this meant he wasn't angry with me anymore.

"Is he here? I know he was in the hospital."

"*Ja*, he is here. You cannot come in. He is recovering."

"Recovering from what? Why didn't you tell me?"

Frouke reared back, insulted. "I do not discuss his business." She tapped the paper in my hand. "You know how to read or not?"

I glared in reply, so she closed the door with a weary shrug.

With shaking hands, I unfolded the paper, worried that I might find angry words. A wave of relief washed over me to see Birdman's slanted handwriting and those first two words: *Little Potato.* I felt like Anne Frank, hidden away in the annex for years, deprived of all treats, and now Frouke had handed me a cake. I wanted to devour it.

Little Potato,

I am sorry. I have been thoughtless and unfair. I have also been unwell and have missed our sessions. But the doctors have fixed me up, and I will soon be as fit as a little hen, and we will discuss the other drawings in the sketchbook you left.

P.S. Thank you for sending the angel. There is no debt between us.

Liefs,

J. Vogelman

I felt so relieved that my muscles went limp. I sank down right there on the doorstep. Birdman wasn't angry with me. Nothing was wrong between us. I still didn't know what had landed him in the hospital, but it couldn't be too bad or Frouke wouldn't have told a joke. Right? I only had to wait while he recovered. Wait and draw.

Chapter 26

From Birdman's I headed up Rock Street and straight to Orion's house. The scare of thinking he'd gone to the hospital had shaken me. I had neglected him for too long.

Javier let me in when I knocked. In the living room, Mrs. Em was sweeping up torn wrapping paper and cut ribbons.

"Merry Christmas Eve!" she said. "We just couldn't wait!"

"Merry Christmas Eve," I said.

"Orion's in there"—she shook her necklace of jingle bells in the direction of the annex—"with his loot."

I popped my head into our secret space, and the moment I saw Orion, I knew I'd messed up—big time. He was bent over his *Cosmos* book, tracing a finger across the star-speckled cover so intently that he didn't even notice me at first. His face was full of longing and disappointment.

"Orion?" I said quietly.

His head shot up, and he shunted the book aside. All vulnerability left him, replaced by a hardness I'd never seen on Orion.

I crept forward, stepping over the presents strewn about. I was an awful friend. I should have been there for him that day he came to tell me about the letter from his dad. I'd been too focused on my drawings for Birdman.

"Merry Christmas Eve," Orion said, but it sounded like an accusation.

"Cool telescope." I gestured to the gift still in its box. The words felt wrong, even as I said them.

"From Javier," Orion grumbled.

The telescope was twice as big as his old one. But the old one was from his dad. I knew he wouldn't want to replace it. It was sacred.

I knelt and put a hand on his arm. "I'm sorry I didn't ask about the letter earlier. Will you tell me about it now?"

It was like I'd let go of a balloon; Orion's air came rushing out, all at once.

"He was going to try to come down for Christmas,"

he said. "Doesn't matter. He called yesterday to say he isn't coming after all. I don't even know if I would have wanted him here."

This was where I was supposed to say the perfect thing to make him feel better, like he always did for me. But "Aw" or "That's too bad" didn't feel like enough. We used to be able to hug each other or shove each other or tie knots and undo them, but none of that seemed right either. Orion needed something more, but I didn't know what it was. Suddenly, after eleven years of friendship, things felt complicated.

"That sucks," I said. *Great, Clara, brilliant insight.*

"Javier's all right. It's just that . . ." Orion trailed off.

I sensed what he wasn't saying. That he wanted to keep his feelings for his dad far away from his feelings for Javier. That if he accepted Javier, he might lose something with his dad. Something more than he'd already lost.

"Feelings are hard to mix?" I suggested.

Orion nodded. "Yeah," he said, "they are."

And then he looked at me with something intense behind his eyes. It was too big and too much, and I wasn't ready to see it. I pulled him into a hug instead. Orion held on tight, his nose buried in my neck. But that felt like too much too. It had been a long time since we'd hugged.

I squirmed away, giggling, and Orion gave me that disappointed look of his.

"Your breath," I said. "It tickled." I rubbed my neck but even later the tingles continued to scurry up my scalp.

Chapter 27

Christmas at my house turned into the Benny show. Halfway through presents, he finally started crawling. He'd been rocking back and forth on his hands and knees for a month, but now, lured by a glittery ornament, he put his arms and legs together, and—*zoom*—he was off!

I had already gotten a book of great Dutch artists from Mom and Dad, but nobody watched me open my big present from Aunt Lindy—a real artist portfolio, huge and made of leather. Everyone was too busy moving ornaments out of Benny's reach. He yanked off the needles instead and shoved a prickly handful into his mouth.

Normally, I would have been annoyed at Benny for hijacking the holiday and at the rest of my family for letting him. But I was too excited about my gift to care. I finally had a beautiful, professional place to keep my drawings, just like a real artist.

Between Christmas and New Year's, I drew my tree every chance I got—with charcoal, chalk pastels, oil pastels, and colored pencils. I was getting close to fifty drawings and looked forward to impressing Birdman with my understanding of the tree.

When my fingers got too cold to hold a pencil, I took a break in the annex with Orion. There seemed to be something new in the air between us. It wasn't discomfort, exactly. We were more careful with each other. The silences between conversation no longer felt natural.

One day, Orion was reading *Cosmos*—really reading it, not just flipping the pages. It looked way too deep for a sixth-grader, but he slogged through it, his tongue poking out the side of his mouth. I was paging through the book of great Dutch artists from Mom and Dad. The beginning showed lots of old-looking landscapes and still lifes and large canvases with somber figures dressed in black. There were portraits too—pages and pages of self-portraits by Rembrandt. Some young, some old, some serious, and some almost mocking.

Maybe Rembrandt was trying to understand himself like I'm trying to understand my tree, I thought as I turned the pages.

Orion's voice pulled me from the book. "Did you know that some stars are so far away and their light takes so long to reach us that by the time we see it, the star has already died?"

"No," I said. "I didn't. I don't like to think I'm gazing up at dead stars."

"Yeah," Orion said, "like we're missing something."

He looked so sad that I turned back to my book, afraid to continue the conversation. I paged through portraits of people with pink cheeks and shiny eyes—all dead now. I came back to a full-page portrait of Rembrandt wearing a floppy black beret, so opposite the crisp black swoop of Rubens's hat in Birdman's atelier.

"These guys are all dead too," I said, laying my book over his. I was trying to spread the sadness around so it would be lighter.

Orion managed a weak smile—for me, not him. "Who is that?"

"Rembrandt." I read from the book: "*He is considered one of the greatest artists in history.*" Wrinkles framed Rembrandt's eyes in the portrait, but out of the shadow of his lid came an amazingly bright twinkle. "Can you imagine him in his studio," I asked, "dabbing that bright spot into his own eye?"

Orion considered.

"Maybe the light from dead stars isn't so sad after all." I started pacing up and down the length of the annex. "And maybe artists don't have to be tortured. Maybe they just have to be crazy enough to send out their own starlight, dab it right into their own eye and send it down through the ages to us so that we can see the light and feel the life and somehow have the courage to make our own dab—on and on so that the light never stops shining."

I stood before Orion with my arms outstretched, breathless from my speech, and really, really wanting him to smile. I didn't know if I was making any sense.

"That's big stuff to think," said Orion, the corner of his mouth twitching.

I squinted at Rembrandt's eye and could see dabs of light from millions of viewers piggybacking on that tiny bright spot.

"The stars and Rembrandt may be dead," I said, "but look at the light they leave behind."

This time Orion's smile was genuine.

That night I tore all my tree drawings out of my sketchbook and spread them around me. I placed and propped my drawings everywhere—carpet, bed, dresser, windowsill—until I sat in the middle of a forest. I wanted to see the big picture.

Jordyn tramped one foot into the room and stopped.

Her bag thumped to the floor. "God, CT, I can't even walk in here."

I started to clear the carpet while Jordyn slouched against the doorframe.

"And get your stuff off my bed," she said, but I noticed she couldn't take her eyes off my drawings.

"What do you think?" I asked.

"Just a bunch of trees."

"But what do you see in them?"

"I see an obsessed little sister who can't keep her stuff on her own side of the room."

But Jordyn no longer stared at my drawings. She stared at me—at my eyes—like she saw a new dab of light there.

Chapter 28

On the last day of the year, things got even weirder with Orion.

I had just finished a tree drawing. For once the sun was out, and fresh light slanted through the branches. I didn't hear Orion's footsteps until he was at my shoulder. I whirled around.

"Geez, you didn't have to ambush me."

He was beaming. "Wanna come in and see my Mars rover? I finished it."

I felt a twinge of disappointment that he'd finished his project before I'd finished mine, but he'd worked so hard that I could genuinely say, "I can't wait."

On our way to the house, Orion slowed down, glancing from side to side. "I wanted to ask you something."

"OK . . . ," I said, matching his seriousness.

He coughed and looked up at the sky. I waited.

"We'll always be friends, right?" He said it with a kind of disappointment.

I didn't know if he was making sure or hoping for something else, but suddenly I was afraid of what he might say next. Afraid that it would change things I didn't want changed. I summoned a laugh and pushed through the back door. "You have to ask?"

In the living room, Mrs. Em was directing Javier, who stood on a chair hanging glittery silver balls from the ceiling for their annual New Year's Eve party. Mom and Dad got all dressed up and attended every year. Jordyn and I stayed home, and Orion always came over to watch the ball drop on TV while we stuffed ourselves with cheese puffs and sparkling cider.

"One more over there," Mrs. Em said, then noticed us. "Pretty classy, don't you think?"

I gave her two thumbs up.

Javier pretended to sag under the weight of the decorations. "Who's doing all the heavy lifting?"

"That's right." Mrs. Em grinned. "Put your back into it."

Orion and I slipped into our secret annex. As promised, his Mars rover was complete. He had set up an obstacle course of cushions and blocks to simulate rocky terrain. With a remote control, he drove the rover through the course, its six wheels rising and falling independently.

"Awesome!" I said.

"Yeah."

I'd thought he would be more excited, but he tossed the remote on a beanbag and stuffed his hands in his pockets. He breathed heavily.

"You OK?" I asked.

"Yup." He jostled his shoulder against mine, like we used to do, only this time it felt tight and awkward. Like trying on a shirt I'd outgrown.

Orion took a deep breath. "You know when you like someone? I mean, *like* like them?"

Oh no, I thought, gulping slowly as my mind raced through the possibilities. *He's going to tell me he likes someone. What if it's me?*

Orion had been acting funny lately—or maybe I had. But I didn't know if I liked him back. I only knew I didn't want to hurt his feelings. And now he was looking at me like he expected something—something more than the look of panic on my face.

Oh, quick, say something, I told myself. But then it hit me: *What if it's not me he likes? What if it's Elise? What if they've been texting each other while she's away in*

California and now he wants to tell me they like each other and everything's going to change?

Somehow that was worse. I tried to make my voice light and breezy. "Nope."

He frowned. "No?"

"No, I don't know what that's like."

"You don't like anyone?"

"Nope."

"Not even a little bit?"

"Not really." It seemed like everybody my age had a crush on somebody, but I wasn't ready for this world of liking people and holding hands and kissing. It felt like another language I didn't understand. Did Orion?

"Oh." He seemed disappointed.

"Do *you* like someone?" The moment the words left my mouth, I wanted to take them back. I would shrivel inside if he said Elise. I would panic if he said me.

I picked up the remote before he could answer. "Let me try this."

I pressed buttons in a frenzy, driving the rover into the wall, then a beanbag, then the other wall. All the while I talked, so that Orion couldn't.

"Did I tell you Benny started crawling? Yeah. He's even more of a monster now. Oops! How do I reverse? There. Got it. And Jordyn saw all my drawings—she pretended to hate them, but I could tell she was impressed. Can you believe it? Jordyn was impressed."

I kept talking and driving wildly until I ran out of things to say. Time to put us both out of our misery. "I have to go. I promised Mom . . . Benny needs . . ."

I banged my shoulder on the annex doorframe on my way out. My feet were on the front doormat and my hand on the knob when Mrs. Em called out to me, "Clara, we'll send Orion over when the party starts."

I froze, my feet glued to the doormat. How would I keep Orion from talking to me about this for the entire evening?

"Watch out!" Javier added. "You might get kissed."

I looked at him in horror. Did he know something I didn't? Automatically my eyes sought Orion's. He had followed me out of the annex and his ears were red, his head bent. A half smile played across his lips.

"Don't mind him," Mrs. Em said. "He means the mistletoe." She pointed above me.

I tipped back my head and saw a clump of mistletoe dangling directly over me. I leapt back and thumped into the door. I had to get out of there or *I* would need the inhaler. With a quick wave to Mrs. Em and Javier, I raced out the door. I hurried across the street, the wind howling after me. My hair lashed my face like punishment for acting like such an idiot. I didn't dare look back, but I hoped Orion wasn't watching from a window.

I was miserable at dinner. My stomach twisted so much I hardly ate a bite. Luckily Mom and Dad were too busy getting ready for the party to notice. For once, I was grateful to be invisible.

But, of course, Jordyn noticed something was wrong. She cornered me in our room. "What's wrong with you?"

"Nothing." I rolled away from her.

"Let's see, you're not eating, didn't say a word at the table, and your face is pasty white. CT, you're not hard to read. I'd say you're scared of something."

I couldn't bear for Jordyn to make fun of me. I clutched my stomach. "I think I'm sick."

Jordyn stood over me, hands on hips. "I'm sure Orion will make you feel better when he comes over later."

"No!" I whirled on her. "I mean, I don't want to see anybody. If he comes over, just tell him . . . tell him—"

"Ah . . . I get it," Jordyn said, giving me a knowing look. "I'll tell him you're really puking your guts out."

"Argh!" I sensed my sister was trying to help, but thinking about things was only making it worse.

"Don't worry. I'll take care of it. And I'll put Benny to

bed. Here." She tossed me her phone and earbuds. "Knock yourself out."

I didn't come out of my room or see Jordyn the rest of the night, but for once, I was grateful for my older sister. There was something between us now. A string—delicate and fine, like a spider's. But strong.

I fell asleep long before midnight, lying on top of the covers with all my clothes on. When I woke the next morning, I discovered that someone had removed the earbuds and covered me with a blanket.

Orion, I learned, had never shown up.

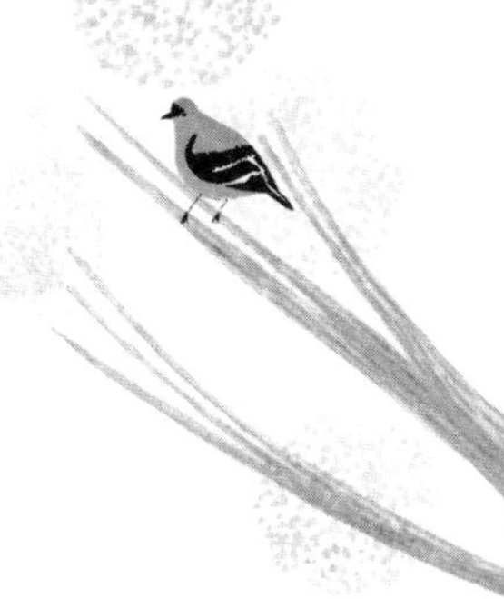

Chapter 29

Three days into the new year, I still hadn't talked to Orion. I'd been drawing the swooping tree every day, but I hadn't gone in to see him, and he hadn't come out to see me.

Now I drew the tree from a new angle—the swooping branch pointing straight at me—using foreshortening to create the illusion of depth. I couldn't concentrate. I kept picturing Orion with red ears and bent head as I stood under the mistletoe. I couldn't figure out what it meant. Was he embarrassed, like I was, at the thought of kissing? Or was it something else?

The hot, panicky feeling rose in me. I knew there were rules about this sort of stuff that everyone but me seemed to know. I could ask Elise, but she was still in California. Besides, maybe it was Elise who Orion liked. She had said he was cute.

I knew I should go talk to Orion. I *wanted* to talk to him. But I'd probably say something idiotic, like when I'd asked him how to get out of my pledge, or hurtful, like when I'd said we should have other friends. I always realized what Orion was feeling a moment too late, after I'd already said the wrong thing.

I got up to move my throne and glanced at the back door. If he came out right now, I could say, "About the mistletoe . . . that was weird."

"Yeah," he'd say, "Javier is crazy."

We'd laugh, and everything would go back to normal.

Or maybe I was overreacting. Maybe this wasn't even a big deal to Orion. Maybe he was happily programming his Mars rover, not even thinking about me.

So why not go see him? I asked myself. But I knew the answer. I didn't have the courage.

School started again, and I began to see my tree everywhere—behind my eyelids, in my dreams. I had easily reached fifty drawings and kept going. The wings I had been sketching turned into trees and the trees into wings.

In class Chloe asked, "Why don't you draw horses anymore? You used to draw such awesome horses. All you do now is trees and wings. No offense, but it's a little weird."

Elise came to my defense. "It's not weird. It's art."

Elise had come back from California different, more friendly—to me at least. With others she was the same aloof Elise. But with me she was warm—draping an arm over my shoulder, leaning in to look at my drawings, steering me in a silly walk through the halls. I guess she missed me.

Still, I didn't talk to her about Orion. I hadn't seen him for days. From a distance, sure. I'd spot him across the cafeteria or on the playground, where he'd started playing wall ball and foursquare. He was more athletic than I'd expected. But we no longer walked to school together. We hadn't looked into each other's eyes since I'd stood under the mistletoe.

Chapter 30

Elise and I spent all day Saturday getting ready for our presentation. Elise had edited the video before I arrived, so at least I didn't have to watch and hear myself over and over again. It was bad enough that I would have to hear it Monday in class.

We uploaded the video, and Elise practiced her lines until she didn't miss any. The only thing left to do was design a Channel Eleven logo, but I couldn't stop thinking ahead to Monday, to the moment I'd have to click *play* and hear my own voice come out of the TV.

"You've already done the hard part!" Elise reminded me. "The rest is icing on the cake." She slid her sketchbook over to me. "This is the part you're good at. What do you think of this for the logo?"

I cringed. She'd tried to make the eleven so fancy that it looked more like dancing snakes than a number.

"Nice," I said and went to work improving it.

Sunday morning, with the sun shining down on me, it happened—understanding.

I was drawing my tree, but my eyes kept searching beyond, to the landscape rolling out behind it. The day was exceptionally clear. I could see our town laid out before me, rolling up the west hill. Past that—the coast range, faded and crumpled as an old pair of jeans. Beyond that, I knew, lay the Pacific Ocean. Across that, the world kept going. Water, shore, mountain, plain, and water again. It didn't stop where I stopped seeing. It kept going.

Behind me, Orion's house loomed. I could feel him inside, waiting. I knew I would have to face him soon. Things had changed, but it wasn't the end. There would never be an end. Only change after change after change. I didn't like it, but there was nothing to do but go with it. I saw that as clearly as I saw the horizon stretching on and on.

I looked down at my half-finished drawing, and finally I understood. Not the tree. Not Orion or Birdman or Elise. What I understood was that I would never be done understanding. There was always more beyond the next mountain range, beyond the next ocean.

I felt as if my dam had broken open and all the stagnant waters came rushing out. I picked up my pencils and tablet. I had to see Birdman—right away.

I collected all my tree drawings, put them in order, and slid them into my leather portfolio. It had been two weeks since Frouke had given me the note from Birdman, and nearly six weeks since I had last seen him. Surely he had recovered by now.

I rapped on the door. A faint *tap-tap-tap* echoed. Was Frouke playing with me? I heard it again. *Tap-tap-tap. BANG!*

Then I realized where the noise had come from—the atelier! Birdman was in there working.

I bounded for the side of the house, but before I took two steps, a meaty hand grabbed my arm and whirled me around.

"I hear him," I said, trying to wrench my arm free. "He's done resting."

"*Ja,*" Frouke said, "he is working. He must not be disturbed."

"I won't disturb him."

"Always you disturb him."

I stopped struggling, and she let go of my arm.

"I don't disturb him." I had thought that after giving me Birdman's note, Frouke might relax her guard. But the evil eye was back. Frouke was not going to budge, and no joke of mine, no matter how funny, would get me through that door.

"He is busy. You go." She pointed a stout finger to the driveway.

I turned, contemplating making a run for the atelier. I was probably faster than Frouke, but the dark foliage circling the house gave me a better idea.

"OK." I tried to sound glum. I walked away with my head down, hoping I wasn't overdoing it. Just before the bend in the drive, I glanced over my shoulder.

Door closed. No Frouke. I ducked into the bushes.

It took a while to creep through the shrubbery. I circled to the side of the house, moving slowly, so that if Frouke happened to look out a window, she wouldn't see suspicious movement. Finally I stood before the atelier.

The light inside shone through the windows and onto the pad of grass just outside. There he was. Birdman. Working. That square of light was the only thing between us. For a moment, I couldn't step into it. I could only watch.

Birdman was skinny—so skinny. As if he'd given up eating. But he didn't look in need of rest. He practically hopped around in excitement, and I knew, without being able to hear, that he was humming to himself.

I gathered my breath, stepped out of the bushes, and crossed the square of light.

"Ah, little potato," Birdman said when I pushed through the door. "You come to see me at last!"

"I *have* been coming to see you," I said. All this time I had assumed he was either too sick or didn't want to see me. It had never occurred to me that he didn't know, that he thought *I* abandoned *him*. "I came every day. Didn't Frouke—?"

At that moment, the door swung open, and Frouke filled the doorway. If she had been a cartoon, steam would have been pumping out of her ears. "Aha!" She pointed a wooden spoon at me.

I hid behind Birdman.

"Frouke, Frouke," Birdman said, gently. "What is the problem?"

"I send her away, but she sneaks back."

Birdman raised his hands slowly and came toward Frouke. "She is here now. She will stay and help me."

"Help you? She distracts you. She makes you remember things you should forget. She makes you angry and sad."

Birdman nodded thoughtfully. "I see."

"It is too painful for you. She must be kept away." Frouke began to usher me out, flicking the wooden spoon as if to sweep me out the door.

Birdman stopped her with a clearing of his throat. "And yet," he said, his voice low and thick, "it is good for me."

I wasn't sure what he meant. What was good for him? Me? The pain? Feeling angry and sad? I was the one who should be angry. All this time, Frouke had kept me away, without telling him I'd been coming. *I* should be giving *her* the evil eye.

But as they stood facing one another—Frouke with her wooden spoon raised and Birdman, looking even skinnier next to her—I saw the way she looked at him. I knew that look—fierce and protective, like she would do anything to shield him from pain. I had to respect that feeling. I had felt it before myself.

Birdman reached out and gently took the wooden spoon from her hands. Without another word, Frouke turned and stalked out the door.

"So?" Birdman said, rubbing his hands together. "Would you like to see my new line of work?"

Now that it was just the two of us, I suddenly felt anxious about showing him my portfolio. A new Birdman stood before me—skinny, energetic, and with a bounce to his step, as if his feet didn't want to touch the ground. His knee didn't buckle anymore. He wasn't the same as the Birdman in my head. With my foot, I slid my portfolio farther under the table.

"Yes," I said, glad to postpone showing him my drawings.

"Already I have five pieces." He disappeared into the storeroom and reappeared with a piece in each hand—one square, one not, both facing away from me. "I took your advice."

I was startled. "What advice?"

"You observed that my latest works were . . . what was the word? Dark? Grim? Unhopeful? So I decided to give a happier new life to these objects that I find."

Birdman paused dramatically, then turned the pieces around. They were faces, playful portraits, each made from the objects in his meticulously organized drawers. In the square one, the facial shape was created with what looked like a bedpan. A small circle for the mouth gave an impression of surprise. The round one was made from a wooden clock. The head of a paintbrush formed a ridiculous goatee.

Birdman's face was just as ridiculous, hovering over his two portraits. Expectant. Boyish. They formed a trio of fools. I burst out laughing.

"I knew it!" he said. "I wanted to make you laugh."

He brought out the rest of the portraits, each one its own character. If I hadn't known better, I never would have guessed they'd been done by the same artist who'd created the swirling painting in the living room. These portraits spoke with a different voice—a voice that gave me courage.

"What's been wrong with you?" I asked.

Birdman's hand patted just below his now-flat belly. "This old body. They've taken out the bad parts. Now I'm healthy as a bear. And I see"—he made a show of peeking beneath the table—"that you have been working too."

I bent to pick up my portfolio. Taking out the bad parts sounded like cancer, but I thought cancer made you lose your hair, and Birdman still had his. He said he was better, and he certainly seemed fine, but still I wanted all the heaps of junk inside him—Chicago, his little bird, sickness, the past—I wanted it all to spill onto the table so I could see it, and we could sort the heaps into compartments.

"Frouke didn't tell me," I said, hanging on to my portfolio. "She didn't even tell me when you came back."

"You mustn't blame Frouke. She only thinks of me."

"What about Chicago?" I asked. "What were you doing there?"

"It is my son who lives there with his family. I'm afraid I have been no better to him than my father was to me. We are stubborn, the men in my family." For a moment, both of his eyes lost their focus, but he brought them back to my portfolio. "Come, let us see."

I held my breath and slipped it across to him. With

ceremony, Birdman slid out the entire stack of drawings and laid his fingertips on top.

"How many?" he asked.

I shrugged. "Sixty?"

He nodded and began to look at them, one by one. My heart drummed like rain on the roof. Birdman gazed at each drawing, sometimes pausing for many moments before turning over the next page. When he came to a quick doodle I did at school, I said, "That one is just—"

"Shhh," he said. "They speak for themselves."

I chewed on a hangnail, seeing the flaws in each drawing, not saying a word. Every so often Birdman would look at me over the brim of his glasses. Each time I felt . . . not good or proud, but seen.

When Birdman came to my last drawing—the one where I'd finally understood—he cleared the other drawings away. I thought he might scold me because the drawing wasn't finished. Instead he looked up. "Now you understand the tree completely?"

My shoulders tried to slump, but I wouldn't let them. *Yes!* I wanted to declare. *I, Clarity Anne Kartoffel, understand the swooping tree completely.* But it wasn't true.

"No," I said, trying to keep my voice steady.

"Why not?"

"Because . . ." If he thought I was wrong, then fine.

I knew what I knew. "Because there's too much. I could keep seeing forever and never get to the end of understanding. If I understood completely, there'd be no point in ever drawing the tree again!"

Birdman's whole face, every crisscrossing crinkle, broke into a deep smile. "Good," he said. "You have swallowed the point."

"You mean, I *got* the point?"

"Yes."

"That was the point?" I said, slightly irritated. "To give me an impossible task and see how long it took before I gave up?"

"Did you give up?"

"No. I guess not. But why did you try to make me think I failed?"

"I had to make sure you digested the point, not just swished it around in your mouth."

"Ew," I said. "I got the point."

"Good," Birdman said with finality. He laid a hand on my stack of drawings. "These are truly wonderful."

"Really?" I couldn't stop a smile from spreading all through me.

"Yes. And this one"—he indicated the last drawing—"this one you will finish, and it will become a painting."

My heart forgot to beat. This was what I had been

working toward. "I'll get to use real artist paint? And brushes? On real canvas?"

Birdman nodded. "Of course," he said. "You are an artist."

"I am," I said, filling up so full of lightness I thought I might float away.

Something new and green unfurled in my chest. Even with all the things going against us—Birdman's sickness, the years between us, the words unspoken—still, Birdman saw what I saw. We had the same feathers. We belonged in the same tree.

"Come," he said, laughing. "We shall build you a canvas."

I stayed in the atelier as late as I thought I could without upsetting my parents. It wasn't until I skipped home under streetlights that seemed to feather on their own that I thought about my secret sketchbook. I hadn't seen it and had forgotten to ask. But I no longer worried about leaving Birdman with no hope. He seemed to have a whole flock of hope-birds singing in his soul.

Chapter 31

On Monday, the morning of the presentation, I woke up and felt my forehead. Darn—no fever. At breakfast, I could barely eat, but that wasn't enough to qualify me as sick. Outside the clouds gathered and pressed close, but rain did not fall.

On the way to school, I spotted Orion walking a block ahead, and my breath quickened. Seeing him, the presentation seemed easy. Talking to Orion—that was hard. But I felt like a real artist now, and he was the first person I wanted to tell.

I quickened my pace, my feet slapping against the pavement. Never mind the embarrassment of New Year's Eve. Never mind everything else. Orion was my best friend.

He rounded a corner, and I started across the street. I would find the right words once I reached him.

Suddenly I stopped, right there in the middle of the

crosswalk. Who was I kidding? I was no good with words. How could I expect to tell Orion what I felt when I didn't even know?

I scurried to the curb, struck by an idea. I was a real artist now. I didn't have to use words. I would use the language I spoke best. With a picture, a gesture, something he could see, I would show Orion what he meant to me.

I continued to school, so busy spinning ideas for my gesture that I forgot to worry about the presentation until Elise squeezed my hands in hers at the door to our classroom. "We can do this," she said.

"Piece of cake," I said with all the false courage I could muster.

We set up the news desk beside the wall-mounted TV screen. Elise put on one of her mom's blazers while I wrapped the Channel Eleven logo I had drawn on butcher paper around the desk. Then I took Ms. Tink's laptop and crawled into my hiding spot under the desk. My job was to click *play* and *pause* at the right times.

It wasn't until I was under the desk, alone with my thoughts, that my jitters took over. I dreaded hearing my slurred voice on the video. I dreaded the sounds that might come from the class—titters, whispers, out-and-out laughter. I wanted to stick my fingers in my ears and block out all of it. I didn't have to worry about these things while making art with Birdman or hanging out with Elise. No one had laughed at my voice for a long time, and I didn't want it to start again.

Elise took her place at the desk, her red high-tops flat on the floor next to where I crouched. A hush fell over the class.

"Hello," said Elise, "and welcome to Channel Eleven News, where we bring you the stories that matter."

The presentation had begun.

Elise ran through the beginning stuff about the war and rations. My finger hovered over the touchpad. Then she said, "Now it's time to join our in-the-field reporter live from the site of a recent bombing."

Elise swiveled her chair, her red shoes tiptoeing toward me. It was time. I moved the cursor into position.

"Monique Silverthorn, can you tell us the situation there?"

I was supposed to click *play*. I knew I had to do it. But my finger wouldn't move. My body clenched, and I froze.

It was such a little thing, a tap with the pad of my finger. I tried to remember how confident I had felt after filming with Elise and Orion. Now it was time to share. Here, now, I could decide to be one person or another. I could decide to be Clarity, the artist, who did every hard thing. Or I could be Clara, who shrank back and didn't talk.

"Monique? Are you there?" Elise's foot moved to kick me.

I scrunched up small, shrinking away from the laptop. My tongue thickened, as if I actually had to speak.

"We seem to be having technical difficulties," Elise said, her foot trying to clobber me.

I heard the frustration in her voice and below it, a note of desperation. I was failing her. This was about more than the presentation. This was about our friendship. I thought of Elise's fragile smile when she'd shown me her dream wall, and something strong surfaced in me. She was counting on me. I had made a pledge.

I ducked past her foot, stretched my arm out long and free, and clicked *play*.

"Hi, Elise." My voice came out of the TV high and tinny. Ugh. I pulled my knees to my chest and pressed my hands to my ears, hoping to smother the quavers in my voice, the slurs of pronunciation.

But it didn't sound like my voice at all. Not the way I heard it in my head. I strained to hear the dryness of my mouth, the flopping of my tongue, the pounding of my heart. But my voice rose with perfect clarity.

"As you can see behind me," I said on the TV, "things are pretty bad here. Most of the people have fled, but those who remain . . ."

My video reporting continued, and Elise interjected here and there with expert timing. I breathed. I listened. There was no laughter from the class. When Elise began her wrap-up, I knew the worst was over.

"Thank you, Monique." Elise's red shoes tapped out a little dance.

"You're welcome, Elise," my TV voice said. I clicked *stop,* still marveling at how normal it sounded.

"That's all we have for you today. This is Elise Van den Berg signing off for Channel Eleven News."

There was a pause, then the classroom erupted with applause. Elise's legs pushed the rolling chair back, and her arm reached down, grabbed my hand, and pulled me out from under the table. It was like coming out of a dark cave. Elise raised my hand above our heads like we were rock stars. She bent us to a bow as everyone clapped.

I wanted to cover my face with hair, but instead I did what Elise had taught me the day she'd joined our class. I looked just over my classmates' heads, to the back wall, at a poster of the beach with seagulls wheeling through the sky. I could almost hear their cries of wind and freedom and triumph.

Chapter 32

The days after the presentation were full of sparkle. Frost coated the grass, windshields, shingles, and sidewalks. Sunlight lit upon the frost and sent out beams of light. Mornings were blinding.

Since Birdman had said I was good for him, Frouke and I had reached a sort of truce. She let me in every day, not just Thursdays. I had finished my tree drawing, the one Birdman said would become a painting. He showed me how to sketch it onto the canvas and coached me on laying in the first swaths of color.

"You must be courageous with your first strokes," he said. "You are painting the feelings and the movement. The essence. Most of it will be painted over anyway, but you must feel it from the beginning."

The tree began to take shape—in colors more intense than real, like the gleam of a memory. That's when it hit me. My gesture for Orion. I hadn't yet decided on what I would do, but now I knew. This was it. What better way to tell him how much I cared about him than a painting of the tree that had been ours since we could toddle around?

I still hadn't spoken to him. I was too afraid of the words: *like, cute, boyfriend* . . . none of those words seemed to fit what I felt.

So instead of talking about my tangle of feelings, I painted them into my tree. The trunk was thick and sturdy. The lower branches arched protectively over the ground. Above I painted twists and unexpected turns, the tip-top branches aching toward the sky. Last I added our swooping branch, a tender curve.

I hoped my gesture would be enough. I hoped he would see what I couldn't say.

If I had looked hard, then, I might have seen the signs. I might have known this soaring couldn't last. But I only saw what was directly in front of me.

One day, as I tossed my backpack on my bed and headed for Birdman's, Mom stopped me at the door. "I wish you'd draw here sometimes, Clara. In the living room or at the dining room table."

She sounded wistful, not mad, but still I felt defensive. "How am I supposed to draw there?" I gestured to the table, covered in half-folded laundry, and to the living room, which was strewn with Benny's toys.

"You're right." Mom sank onto the couch. "I know you're learning a lot with Mr. Vogelman. I just miss seeing you drawing. It makes me so proud."

I was stunned. Mom was always so busy, I'd assumed she was glad to have me out of her hair. "I can show you some of my sketches, if you want?"

Mom smiled. "I'd like that."

So, while Benny napped, I showed Mom my whole portfolio of trees. I told her about seeing the essence and about understanding—I even told her about joking with Frouke and Birdman's new face collages.

"You know," said Mom, "I remember the first time I met Mr. Vogelman."

"Really?" I held my breath. I used to love Mom's stories. She would stop picking up toys or writing shopping lists to talk to me. I would climb onto her lap, press my cheek to her chest, and feel the vibrations of her voice.

But things had changed since Benny was born. Now I just hoped he wouldn't cry and ruin the story.

"You were almost a year old," she said. "Your father was busy with his new job, but I wanted to get to know the neighborhood, so I packed you onto my back, took Jordyn by the hand, and knocked on every door. Mrs. Davenport gave me some iris bulbs she'd just dug up. Mrs. Emerson invited me in for coffee, and you clobbered Orion in his crib. Oh, I was so embarrassed."

I smiled at the familiar story, wistful for the days when a fight could be solved with a teething cracker and a jangly toy.

"Everyone made me feel so welcome. Until I got to the end of the street. When I knocked, that dour woman opened the door. Even ten years ago, she looked old." Mom laughed. Each word of hers was the stroke of a brush that, layer after layer, painted a picture so vivid it could be my own memory. "She barely spoke English, but she let me know very clearly that Mr. Vogelman was working and could not stop to say hello."

Good old Frouke.

"I took you girls back every day that week—and the next. I was determined to meet the mysterious Mr. Vogelman. Finally she let us in. By then I was sure he would be arrogant and unfriendly."

I perched on the arm of the couch, desperately wanting Mom to like him.

"But when he greeted us, I couldn't dislike him."

I let out a breath. "Why not?"

She reached out and gently smoothed back my hair with both hands. "Because of you."

"Me?"

Mom smiled. "When Mr. Vogelman saw us, he stared as if we had come to visit him out of a dream. He didn't say hello—just stared. Finally he snapped out of it and introduced himself and welcomed us to the neighborhood and all that. He was quite friendly."

Exactly what I had thought when I first met him. Why did all the neighborhood stories make him sound mean?

"And you," Mom continued, "you reached out your little hand to him, and he held his finger up for you to grab. 'Such long fingers,' I remember him saying. 'Perhaps she will be an artist.' 'Or a musician,' I said. But, of course, we didn't know about your hearing problem then."

From down the hall came Benny's waking-up-whimpers. But I wasn't ready for the story to be over. "What else did he say?"

"I don't remember."

Benny wailed for real, and just like that, the spell was broken. But Mom didn't go to him right away.

"Come here for a sec." She held me by the shoulders. There were tears in her eyes.

"What's wrong, Mom?"

"Nothing. My girls are growing up, that's all. Give me a kiss."

I guessed there never was an end to understanding, even for adults. She kissed me as she hadn't done since I was little—right on the lips.

Chapter 33

At Birdman's, as I swished my paintbrush through the water-filled Mason jar or mixed a new color on my palette, I kept thinking about Mom's story. It was a warm feeling to know that Birdman and I had connected before—before the glass ball, before I ever saw his painting. I wondered if he remembered that moment, my fingers wrapped around his, if he remembered baby-me.

"How does it look?" I asked.

"That does not matter so much at this point. You are getting the feel. You are making choices. Each choice leads you into a different painting. You are not walking a path, taking one step and then the next—you are doing and seeing everything at once. You must paint the entire painting with each stroke of your brush. Be bold. Be free. Do not make teeny, tiny marks."

"I need a break," I said. And to figure out what the heck he was talking about.

"Yes." Birdman said. "Always you must step back. Refresh your eyes. Come back and see anew."

I wandered into the main part of the house, stopping to look at the swirling painting, which still captivated me, when something new caught my eye. On the table by the armchair sat a silver frame with a photograph inside.

It was a modern studio portrait of a family: a skinny mom, a sandy-haired dad, and three children. The oldest girl looked about my age. Suddenly I recognized the smile, the eyes. She wasn't wearing braids now, but this was the girl from the photo I had dropped. Birdman's little bird. My eyes jumped back to the parents. One of them had to be Birdman's son or daughter.

"Snooping again?" Frouke said behind me.

I turned slowly, summoning the courage to face her evil eye. I hoped she wouldn't be wielding a wooden spoon. But there was no evil eye. No wooden spoon. Just Frouke with her straight mouth.

"This picture wasn't here before," I said. "Where did it come from?" I don't know why I hoped she would tell me. She never answered my questions.

But then, like a miracle in a movie, a ray of light

slanted in from the window and laid itself at my feet. Frouke looked me over. Finally she nodded to herself and said, "The wife send it."

"So, the man in the photo is . . . ?"

"*Ja,* he is the son of Joris Vogelman."

Joris. Birdman's first name was Joris. Strange that I hadn't known that before. I looked back at the photo, to his little bird, the granddaughter he missed. I thought of the story my mother had told me about meeting Mr. Vogelman. How he had stared at me—my little hand wrapped around his finger. Perhaps I had reminded him of his granddaughter.

Surprisingly, Frouke was on a roll. She clucked her tongue and said, "He don't tell them he is sick. He don't say he has operation. The Vogelman men are too proud. So, I write to wife, and she send photograph."

She switched on her evil eye and bore down on me, shaking a finger as hard as any wooden spoon. "But you must not tell him I write to wife. You promise?"

"I promise," I said, still in shock that she'd told me as much as she had.

"*Goed,*" she said, and the word sounded like she was about to hock a loogie at me.

I went back to the atelier. Birdman was right. I did see with fresh eyes. But it wasn't my painting that

I saw anew—it was Birdman. His colors had changed, deepened.

"And what do you see now?" he asked, looking at my painting.

I didn't take my eyes off him. "Everything at once."

Chapter 34

The next day, Birdman said, "Come, I have something to show you." He practically soared to one of his junk drawers—clearly recovered from whatever illness had plagued him—and pulled out two old-fashioned bicycle bells. "These will make a fun portrait, don't you think?"

In answer, I pressed down on the thumb pad. The bell erupted in a shrill ring that echoed through the atelier. I let the sound subside. My eyes met Birdman's. His thumb moved to the pad of the other bell.

"One," he said, "two, three."

We rang the bells over and over again. Joyous ringing filled my ears, filled the atelier, filled us both. Finally the last trill of sound faded. Silence fell around us like snow. We let it settle.

"There is a Dutch word," Birdman said. "*Zwijgen.*

It means 'to remain silent.' But it is different from the English. It is a work-word. How do you say it? A verb. Like *running* or *jumping* or *singing.*"

"So, it's like not saying anything?" I asked.

"Not quite. You say, 'I am silent. You are silent. We are silent.' In Dutch, I *zwijg,* you *zwijgt,* we *zwijgen.* In English it is something you *are.* In Dutch it is something you *do.*"

I didn't get the difference, but I nodded slowly. Maybe it would come.

Birdman put the bells away. "They will wait for the right portrait. Now we make one together."

"A portrait?"

"Of course. We must have a subject. Who shall it be?"

I thought of his little bird, but immediately dismissed the idea. "We could do one of you."

"Hmm," he nodded. "A self-portrait. What an idea."

Just then a quick *rap-rap-rap* sounded at the door.

"*Ja?*" Birdman called.

Frouke poked in her head. "I hear alarming noises." She narrowed her eyes at me. "Everything is OK?"

A smile of inspiration swooped onto Birdman's face. I caught the inspiration too, and we both looked at Frouke's broad forehead and straight mouth poking around the door.

Birdman nudged me and assumed a serious pose. I stifled a giggle.

"Frouke," he said, "what noises did you hear?"

Frouke shifted her weight but stayed partway behind the door, hesitant to enter fully. "It sound like bells."

"Bells?" Birdman asked.

"*Ja,*" said Frouke. "The bells of my girlhood. Riding along the dike to school. The wind in my back. My bicycle bell singing for joy."

But Frouke's face was the opposite of joyful. It was full of pain and longing. For the first time, I wondered why she'd left her home to come here. The thought of living anywhere but Rock Street made me twist inside.

"Do you need anything of me?" Frouke asked.

"No, thank you," Birdman said, sober now. "You've given us everything we need."

As soon as she closed the door, we got to work on our portrait.

"Frouke's face is square," Birdman said, "so we must start with a block." He brought out block after block of wood and laid them out on the table.

"Too smooth," I said, dismissing one.

"Too narrow," Birdman said of the next.

Too brittle. Too soft. Too hard. We rejected one after another. Finally we found one that had been painted a pasty-white color. Little bumps showed beneath the paint.

"That's her mole." I pointed to the largest bump—discolored but yielding.

"We must not forget the compassion," Birdman said.

I understood. Despite Frouke's evil eye and elephant blockade of the front door, despite all my failed jokes, I was beginning to *see* her.

For a while, we worked in silence, digging through drawers, hunting for that perfect straight line to describe her mouth. And what to evoke those narrow eyes? Bent bottle caps? And the snub of the nose. A button? A drawer knob?

When we decided on all the parts, it was time to stop for the day. I lingered in the doorway.

"Something more?" Birdman asked.

I had promised not to tell Birdman that Frouke had been in contact with the wife, but that didn't mean I couldn't mention the family picture. "I saw the new photo in the living room."

"Ah," Birdman said, smiling a smile of deep sadness. "My son's family."

"The little bird you went to visit?"

Birdman let out a sigh, like the winter giving way to spring. "Tandy, the girl of my heart. I knew it from the first moment I met her. She was only a baby. You never saw such bright eyes. Taking in everything. The eyes of an artist." His droopy eye stared out the window. "She is your age now."

I thought of my mother's story, of my tiny hand wrapped around Birdman's finger. That could have been Tandy. She could have been here with him now, instead of me.

"What happened in Chicago?" I whispered.

"Again my son and I quarreled. He says one artist in the family is enough. It is not the life he wants for his daughter. He wants no contact. It was the same with my wife." Birdman sank to a stool, took off his glasses, and pinched the bridge of his nose. "I was not an easy man to live with. Apparently, I have not changed."

I wished I could wrap my hand around his finger again. I wished I was his little bird so I could stop his heart from breaking. Instead I said, "But there is a new photograph in your living room now."

He smiled. "So there is."

"And always there must be hope," I said. "The viewer brings the hope, remember?"

"*Ja*," he said. Birdman tapped our Frouke on her wooden chin. "Next time we assemble her?"

"Next time," I said, thinking we had an infinite

string of next times ahead. If I had looked hard, then, I might have seen the signs. I might have known this soaring couldn't last. But I only saw what was right in front of me.

Chapter 35

Birdman's story about his son and granddaughter filled me with urgency. I had never realized that something you loved could slip away so easily.

All day Saturday, I worked to finish my painting of the swooping tree for Orion. I was close, but something was missing.

Birdman took a break from screwing in Frouke's nose and came over to look. "Sometimes we let them sit," he said, "to discover themselves. And to make our own eyes forget."

"I don't have time to let it sit." I didn't want more to slip away.

"It is a very fine painting of a tree."

"But I want it to be more than that."

"Ah, then you must tell a story."

"A story?"

"Yes. You see how these top branches disappear into the sky? What does that mean? And what does this branch"—he pointed to the swooping one—"say to the viewer? To you? Is it an invitation?"

I nodded. This tree was the story of us—Orion and me. The branches disappeared into the sky because that part of our story wasn't yet told. "I know what I'm going to do."

"Then I get out of your way."

With feathery-light strokes, I added figures—Orion and me crawling in the tall grass, chasing each other around the trunk, sitting on the swooping branch with legs dangling. Once I had painted us from every memory I could think of, I painted what never happened, what was only hope. I painted us climbing up to the tip-top branches, and then, in the sky above, I painted the faint whisper of wings.

When I stood back, I was pleased with the effect. There was none of the worry I felt on the surface when I thought of Orion and Elise and what would happen if they liked each other more than me. This was a stronger feeling, deep and abiding.

"It is love," said Birdman, leaning in to look. "You love this tree, and you love everything around it."

I squirmed under the weight of the word. I wasn't ready for the big, wide world of grown-up romance it suggested.

Birdman seemed to read my mind. "Love is not one shape. It is not always a red heart. Sometimes it is a tree. Or a bird. Or a bicycle bell." He rang the bell that sat on the worktable with the other objects awaiting new life.

I couldn't help laughing. I figured that if I'd never be done understanding my tree, I surely would never be done understanding love. That was OK. My gesture for Orion was ready.

Sunday morning, while Orion and Mrs. Em were at church, I snuck over to his house—Javier let me in—and hung my painting in the annex, right in the center. Then I stepped back to admire it, big and bold against the bare wood.

I imagined Orion walking in and stopping in his tracks when he saw it. *I'm sorry for acting weird,* it would say. *I hope I haven't hurt your feelings. This is us. Let's trust each other and be brave.*

I still hadn't spoken to him. Maybe he was mad at me for running away on New Year's Eve. Maybe he was avoiding me because he was embarrassed. I remembered his red ears, his bent head, and that half smile. Suddenly I was certain he liked me. The thought filled me with a warm, fluttery feeling.

I imagined that goofy smile spreading across his face, my gesture untangling the weirdness that had knotted itself between us. We wouldn't have to say a word.

I climbed onto my roof, settling my back against the chimney, to watch for Orion coming home. My plan was to show up a few minutes after he arrived, giving him time to see my big gesture.

I would draw the bird tree while I waited, I decided. I hadn't seen the finches in days, possibly weeks. I wondered when they'd return. I opened my sketchbook, and with quick, light strokes, I sketched the spindly outermost branches. With the side of my pencil, I thickened the branches, gave them strength.

I'd been up on the roof for an hour when Mrs. Em's green Subaru turned down Rock Street and swung into her driveway. My stomach fluttered and swooped. But only Mrs. Em got out. No Orion.

Sometimes Orion stayed for youth group, I remembered. That had to be it.

I went back to sketching. Clouds gathered overhead—darker, closer. Rain was coming.

I was on my third drawing of the bird tree when my ears pricked up. A sound—like a tinkling laugh—came from the head of Rock Street. Not an Orion-sound. But familiar.

It was Elise. That was her letting-her-guard-down laugh.

A moment later, she and Orion came into view. I watched them walk down the street together, laughing, talking, bumping shoulders.

Suddenly I knew I'd misinterpreted everything. Orion didn't like me. He liked Elise.

My insides knotted. So they liked each other. So what? Did I even want him to like me?

The knots pulled tighter and tighter.

Together, Elise and Orion disappeared into his house. A drop of rain hit my cheek, and the knots unraveled. *I* unraveled. All the certainty I'd felt when I hung the painting spooled out of me, and I felt lost and alone and stupid.

Another raindrop hit my forehead. Elise was going to ruin my big gesture just by being there. Birdman had said it was love, but that word felt too big and foolish and dagger-sharp. I had to take my gesture back before Orion saw it.

I stood up straight—something I never did when I was on the roof—without a thought to the placement of my feet. A loose shingle shot out from under my foot, and I thumped down hard on my tailbone. I threw my arms around the chimney to keep from sliding, and my cheek scraped against the brick. Off came my glasses. They skittered down the shingles and hopped over the edge of the gutter. It seemed a long time before I heard the *crack* on the front walk.

At that moment, the sky opened. At first it sent down a smattering of drops, but they quickened, pinging and pelting. I scooped up my sketchbook and pencil case and scampered down to the sundeck. Mom always said to go down the ladder-stairs backward, but I never did. On the first step, I slipped. My sideways momentum carried me over the rail and down into the laurel hedge, butt-first.

For a moment, I lay there, sticks poking me in every direction. I couldn't get my breath. Then my lungs filled with air, and I flailed my limbs until I tumbled out of the hedge to go half-limping, half-running across the street.

I burst into Orion's house.

"Hi, Clara." Without my glasses, Javier was a smudge waving from the armchair. "What happened to you?"

My throat was so tight I couldn't swallow. I shook my head, biting back the roar building inside me.

"They're in there, honey," Javier said.

I knew without seeing that he meant the annex. *Why would he bring her there?*

I pushed through the door. Two blurry faces turned to me in surprise, the Christmas lights dancing over their heads. I squinted but saw no look of guilt, no caught-in-the-act surprise. Instead they looked delighted to see me.

"Clara!" said Orion.

"We were just talking about you!" said Elise. "We saw your painting and were like—"

I cut her off. "It was a mistake." I couldn't bear to hear what they thought of it. I pushed past and grabbed my painting off the wall.

"What happened?" Elise tried to reach out to me, but I used the painting as a shield. "You've got sticks and leaves in your hair. And your clothes are soaked."

"Where are your glasses?" Orion asked. "Your cheek is bleeding!"

I didn't care about any of that. I only wanted to get out of there before I was asked to explain more of my stupidity. I couldn't believe Orion had brought Elise here.

I turned on her. "You don't belong here!" I must have shouted because they both drew back.

A silence fell, heavy and hard. I made for the door, but Orion blocked my escape, standing firm.

"What did you expect?" he asked. "You said I should have other friends. Now I do, and you're mad? I should be the mad one."

"What do *you* have to be mad about? This is *our* sacred space!"

Orion flung out his arms, and his eyes flashed. "Were you ever going to tell me about Mr. Vogelman?"

For a moment, I couldn't catch my breath. He was right, but I buried that thought—along with all the other ways I'd been wrong—and glared at Elise. She must have told him.

"Friends tell each other—" Orion began, but I couldn't stand to hear more. I let out what had been building inside me. With a roar from my deepest, most animal place, I pushed Orion. With the flat of the painting. On the chest. With all my might.

He fell into the table and thumped hard against the wall. The lamp tipped to the floor.

Orion's breath began to hitch. Elise bent to help him up.

The shock of what I'd done hit me like a blast of air in the face. I clapped a hand over my mouth, but there was nothing left to come out. I didn't wait for Elise to say something. I didn't squint to see Orion's eyes. I turned and fled.

I heard Javier's distant, "Clara . . ." as I barreled through the living room and dashed out the door, into the rain.

By the time I made it across the street, my shoes were soaked and rivulets flowed through my hair, down my neck, under my collar. Water had seeped into the canvas.

It didn't matter that the painting was probably ruined. I'd already ruined my big gesture anyway.

My limbs trembled as I made my way up the front walk. I found my glasses with my foot—*crunch!*

As I bent to pick up the pieces, something white caught my eye where I had fallen into the hedge. Coming closer, I found my sketchbook, its pages spread like wings, as if it had tried to take flight and failed. I folded the soaking pages back between the cardboard covers, poured the water from my pencil case, and went inside.

I dripped all the way down the hall, hoping Jordyn was not in our room. No such luck. She gave me a long look in the mirror of her vanity as I dumped my armload on the floor and flopped onto my bed.

"What happened?" Jordyn asked.

"It's Orion and Elise—" I broke off. She probably only wanted to know so she could make fun of me.

"Ah," she said, with a knowing smile. "Jealous, huh?"

"No." I huffed.

"It's OK to be jealous," she said. "I've been jealous lots of times."

"I am *not* jealous."

"Whatever you say."

Jordyn rose, and I thought she was coming to hug me, but she walked out of the room.

Carefully I separated a few pages of my sketchbook—completely soaked. The pencil and charcoal had run and faded. At least it wasn't my secret sketchbook—that was still safe at Birdman's—but I was surprised to look at the ruined drawings and feel nothing. Maybe the rain had washed all my feeling away.

Jordyn returned and threw a towel at me, then bent to wipe the water off my painting.

"I think it'll survive." She picked up the pieces of my glasses. "I'll tell Mom you tripped and fell."

Her face was soft and blurred around the edges, the way I remembered her looking when we were much younger and I didn't talk. I draped the towel over my head, grateful again for my sister.

Chapter 36

I didn't have backup glasses, so Mom called the eye doctor and ordered a new pair. It would take a few days.

Fine with me. I didn't want to see anyway.

Without glasses, the world was a different place. Blurry, of course, but also more dreamlike. Anything might happen. But only what happened on the inside felt real.

I was zipping up my backpack, one tine at a time, when Mom handed me Orion's note—a tight triangle, intricately folded. I stared at it, knowing I'd acted horribly, knowing I needed to say *sorry sorry sorry* until my voice turned hoarse. But I couldn't face him, not after what I'd done. Not with that hard pit of betrayal still lodged inside me.

I slipped Orion's note into my back pocket and ignored it.

Mom put her hand on my shoulder and said, "If you want to talk . . . ," but I ignored that too.

In class, I ignored Elise, who kept turning in her seat to catch my eye. The details of her expression blurred to nothing.

It was raining so hard we couldn't be outside that day at recess, so I ran to the far corner of the covered area and tucked myself against a post, trying to be invisible. I watched the rain come down in heavy sheets, listening to its drum on the roof, as if it could hammer this miserable feeling out of me.

I wasn't jealous. I just didn't like what was happening. Why did it have to be one way or another? Why couldn't there be a million ways to like someone?

I slid Orion's note out of my pocket. He always said the right thing.

The end was secured so tightly that I had to rip it open. The note read:

YOU DON'T GET ALL OF ME

—O

I stared at the words as if they were pieces from different puzzles that wouldn't fit together. My face burned with shame. I held the note away from my body. Drops of rain pit-patted on the paper, batting it down. I crumpled it and tossed it into a little river running through the bark chips and down the hill. The water carried the note away.

"Littering, I see," said a voice beside me. It was Elise, and she had me cornered—hands on hips, eyes blazing. "Clarity Kartoffel, what is your problem?"

That was the question, wasn't it? I wanted to curl up like a potato bug.

"I thought I'd give you the morning to apologize," she continued, "but now there's no excuse."

Shame washed over me. "I'm sorry, Elise," I said. "I shouldn't have—"

"I'm not talking about me!" she interrupted. "I'm tough enough to handle a little shouting. It's Orion you hurt."

The truth of her words hit me like a smack in the face. I didn't deserve Orion. I knew I'd hurt him—not only by shoving him, but by ignoring him. By taking him for granted.

But instead of saying that, I said, "He hurt me too," and shouldered past Elise.

I ran straight across the covered area, straight through the blur of ball games—wall ball, basketball, four-square. Balls and limbs and faces came at me from every direction.

"Hey!" I heard.

"What do you think you're doing?"

"Get off the court!"

A ball hit me in the shoulder. Another bounced off my thigh, but I didn't care. I wanted to be battered and pelted. A heavier ball hit me on the side of the face, and I threw up my arms and ran.

Finally I made it to the bathroom, crashed into a stall, and slid the lock. I tried to slow my breathing. I felt the tender spot on my cheekbone—definitely bruised. I crouched in the stall, tipping my head to the buzzing fluorescent lights, letting them sear my eyes, not even trying to feather the light.

A moment later, the bathroom door creaked open.

"Clarity." Elise's voice had a new layer of softness.

I held my breath. Her shoes squeaked on the smooth concrete.

"I know you're in there," she said. "I can see your shoes."

I remembered the time I had come upon Elise sniffling in the bathroom. That seemed like years ago. Now it was me closing myself in a stall. I knew Elise wasn't going to lose courage and leave, like I had.

"Come out and let's talk."

My nose began to run, but I would not sniff. I swiped with my sleeve.

"At least let me look at your face. I saw that basketball hit you."

"I broke my glasses," I said, as if that explained it.

The first bell rang.

"Clarity, I'm your friend. What's the point if you can't trust me?" There was a note of frustration in Elise's voice.

But I didn't trust her. I didn't trust Orion. I didn't trust myself—what I knew or what I thought I knew.

"Do you like Orion?" I blurted out.

"What?"

"Do you like Orion? You said he was cute."

"Is that what this is all about?" There was a smile in Elise's voice that made me feel foolish. "Come out and let me tell you something."

I shook my head. Stupid, since I knew she couldn't see me through the door. I couldn't seem to stop doing stupid things.

"Fine, I'll tell you from out here." Elise stepped close. I could see the toes of her shoes under the door and her mouth close to the crack. "Orion likes you," she whispered. "And unless I'm a terrible judge of these things, you like him too."

At that, I burst out crying—big, blubbery tears and gut-hollowing sobs. Out went all the shame and worry and betrayal I'd been feeling. In came relief at the truth of her words. And laughter at how ridiculous I'd been.

I realized that things had changed long before the moment under the mistletoe, long before I had found out Orion was friends with Elise. Things had started to change when I stepped into Birdman's house, when I started spending afternoons there instead of with Orion, when I embarked on my journey to become a real artist.

Things had changed because of *me*.

I had changed.

Why shouldn't Orion change too?

I unlatched the door and came out. Elise folded me into her arms.

Just then, the bathroom door swung open. Elise and I froze, our arms still round each other, my face wet with tears. I didn't need my glasses to recognize Ms. Tink. I braced myself for harsh words and no exceptions. I knew the second bell was about to ring.

In a voice wholly different from her teacher voice, Ms. Tink said, "Sorry to disturb you, ladies. I only need to wash my hands."

We gaped while she washed.

"Elise, you'd better take Clara to the nurse's office when you're finished here," she added. "Get her face looked at."

With that, Ms. Tink left. I stared after her. I never thought she'd surprise me with kindness.

As we walked back to class with a hall pass from the nurse and an ice pack on my face, Elise said, "Did you know that my name means 'from the mountain'?"

"Elise?"

"No. Van den Berg."

"Oh." I didn't know why she was telling me this.

"I've always imagined myself like that. Not like I used to live on a mountain, but that I'm actually made from pieces of mountain. Like the mountain is my dad. Like it's something inside me that no one can take away."

We turned down the sixth-grade hallway.

"You've got to have something inside you that no one can take away," Elise continued.

I thought of Anne Frank and all the things inside her that she put into words. I thought of my secret sketchbook drawings. I thought of the wings I kept seeing and drawing. Maybe I knew what Elise meant.

"My name means 'potato,'" I said.

"What?"

"My last name—*Kartoffel*. It means 'potato' in

German." I didn't know why I was telling her except that it seemed like the right thing to say.

"Potato? Your name is Clarity Potato?" A smile played around Elise's lips, but I didn't mind.

"Clarity Anne Potato to you," I said.

She giggled. "That's sure something no one can take away from you."

Chapter 37

I didn't know if Elise was right about me liking Orion, but I did know that Birdman was right about love. I had a tree-shaped love for Orion inside me, and I needed to talk to him right away.

At lunchtime, I looked for him in the cafeteria, but Orion didn't arrive with the rest of his class. I dragged Elise with me to check the gym. No Orion. We checked his classroom, then the playground, but we couldn't find him anywhere.

"Maybe he doesn't want to be found," Elise tried to tell me.

That afternoon I kept asking for the bathroom pass so I could peer in the windows of Orion's classroom. Seeing the blurry back of his head was like pressing on a bruise. It hurt, but I kept doing it anyway.

When I got back to my classroom after my third

bathroom pass, Ms. Tink called me to her desk. "Clara, you're to go to the office."

Oh, no. Somebody must have seen me lurking outside Orion's classroom.

But Ms. Tink smiled. "Bring your things. Your mom is here to pick you up."

I gathered my things, relieved not to be in trouble, but confused. Why would Mom pick me up half an hour before school was over? I tossed a puzzled shrug in Elise's direction, hoping she got it. Everything was a blur.

In the office, Mom was bouncing a fussy Benny on her hip. "Hurry up, we're going to be late."

"Late for what?" I asked.

She nudged my shoulder to steer me out the door and across the parking lot. "For the eye doctor. We have to pick out your new frames."

"But . . . I can't," I stammered. "I need to—"

"Clarity, this is the only time that works for me. Since when are you upset about getting out of school early?"

She didn't really want an answer, so I got in the car and slammed the door while she wrestled Benny into his car seat. I'd have to wait to talk to Orion.

At the doctor's office, a time bomb ticked inside me as I tried on one pair of glasses after another.

"The purple ones are cute," Mom said, "but I kind of like these blue ones. Too bold, you think?"

"They're fine," I said. "I like them." Seeing Orion was the only thing that mattered.

"What about these?" The lady helping us held up another pair.

I suppressed my groan and squinted at the clock. School was out by now. Orion would be home.

Finally, just as Benny tried to pull over a potted plant, we settled on the first pair I'd tried on. But then we had to pick Jordyn up, and then Mom needed to make a "quick stop" at the grocery store, and by the time we got home it was nearly dark, and everyone was cranky. I dropped my stuff, headed straight to Orion's house, and thumped on the door. The rain had come and gone, but dark clouds still gathered on the horizon.

Mrs. Em answered, still wearing her coat. She must have just arrived home too. "I'm sorry, Clara. He doesn't want to see you right now."

The words from Orion's note gonged around inside me: *You don't get all of me.* At that moment, I didn't want any of him. All I wanted was to give him a piece of myself, to show him that I wasn't as silly and stupid as I'd been acting, to show him that I would do anything for him.

"I'll tell him you came by."

The voice inside me was screaming. *That isn't all! There's so much more!*

"Maybe try again tomorrow morning?"

There was nothing left to do but nod. Yes, I would do that. I would get up early. We would walk to school together like we used to.

Mrs. Em closed the door sadly and left me on the porch, defeated. My whole day had been building to the moment I could speak to Orion, and now that moment had been skipped over.

I was going to go home, but a childish urge took hold of me, and I went to the swooping tree instead. I climbed up and let its curve cradle me, feeling sorry for myself. Poor Clarity. The wind picked up and shook large droplets loose. They splatted down like great tears.

I would stay here all night. I would stay until I saw Orion. Maybe he would see me from a window and come out.

But I heard no creak of the back door opening, no footsteps coming across the lawn.

It was Jordyn who eventually came, not Orion. "Time to come home, CT."

I let her lead me, feeling like gravity had doubled on me. My limbs felt heavy, my head thick as she brought me to the living room and sat me down on the couch next to Mom. Benny was already in bed.

"You're shivering," Mom fussed, wrapping a blanket around me and rubbing my shoulders.

I squinted at the clock. It was just after six o'clock, but I was so tired, as if months of events had happened in one day.

Dad joined us and sat forward with elbows on his knees. Jordyn turned her face away as if someone was about to rip off a Band-Aid.

"Do you want to talk about what's bothering you?" Mom asked.

Jordyn snorted.

"You're not helping," Mom scolded.

"Well, excuse me, but you aren't either," Jordyn said. "Since when has CT ever wanted to *talk?*"

Good old Jordyn. She wouldn't let Mom and Dad cheer me up.

"Just tell her," Jordyn said to Mom.

Tell me what? My brain thought the words, but my mouth was too weary to say them.

"We have bad news," Mom said. "I hate to tell you when you're already upset . . ."

"But we knew you'd want to know right away," Dad finished for her.

"Your friend," Mom said, "he was admitted to the hospital this afternoon. I didn't find out until we got home. I'm sorry you didn't get a chance to talk to him before. . ."

"What?" Had something happened to Orion while I was picking out glasses? An asthma attack?

"Sweetie," Dad said, "what your mom is trying to say is that he died. This evening."

My parents' faces came into sharp focus. The word *died* chimed through my head.

"It was very sudden," Mom added. "The doctors say he wasn't in much pain."

Pain? A slimy lump of panic rose in my throat. It made no sense. Mrs. Em had acted like Orion was right upstairs.

"He can't be," I croaked. "I saw him at school. Mrs. Em said . . . I didn't get a chance to . . ."

"Oh, no, sweet pea. No." said Mom, coming to wrap her arms around me. "Not Orion."

"Not Orion?" I breathed.

"Orion's fine." Mom rubbed circles on my back.

"Orion's not dead?" I had to make absolutely sure.

"Of course not." Dad pulled one of his exaggerated faces. "What made you think that?"

I ignored his question. "Then who . . ." In a flash, I knew. "Birdman."

"Birdman?" Dad looked even more confused, but Mom took my hands in hers, looked me in the eyes, and said, "Frouke just called to tell us."

It all sank in, but I didn't want to believe it. I had just seen him on Saturday. I had painted, and he had worked on Frouke's portrait.

My mind and my mouth weren't working together. Nothing was working together. I shook my hands in front of me like shaking off water. There was no time to breathe, no time to cheer that Orion was alive. Orion and Birdman and sorrow smeared together in my mind like a finger painting where the colors swirled until they were mud.

I tried to stand and hands reached out to me. I don't know what happened next except that I felt empty and lost.

Later my parents told me I said, "He can't be dead. He has wings."

Later they told me I kept shaking my head, saying, "No, no, no . . ."

Later they told me Birdman had colon cancer, and they thought I knew. They used the word *relapse* and said there was nothing the doctors could do.

But I remember little of that night—not the sounds coming from me, not what I did, not how I got to bed. It was as if my senses refused to record anything. My vision blurred more and more, probably from tears, until I saw nothing, and no matter how hard I squinted at the overhead lights or the lamps or the streetlight out my window, I could not feather the light.

Chapter 38

The next day, Mom let me stay home from school. I stayed in bed all morning, falling in and out of sleep. Each breath was a new, hard thing I had to force myself to do. When awake, I stared at the ceiling, grateful that I couldn't see clearly. Seeing made me think of Birdman.

Later, I moved to the living room and watched TV, sitting inches from the screen. The characters filled my vision so I didn't have to think about anything.

But of course, thoughts crept in.

If only I'd known, I could have seen Birdman before he died.

And I thought of Orion. Of course he didn't want to see me after I'd shoved him and ignored him and treated him like an on-demand station. How could he like me when I'd only done things to hurt him? He was as lost to me as Birdman.

On Wednesday Mom made me go to school. I told Elise about Birdman, and she stuck close, trying to lift me up. Even the smallest things—breathing, walking, sitting—were too much for me. Everything surpassed my courage.

At lunch Elise kept saying, "Clarity, take a bite," and when the bell rang, she said, "Time to get up," and tugged my arm.

A couple of times I saw Orion from a distance. One time I thought he waved, but everything was out of focus, and there was a little pinch inside me, but it felt like the memory of a pinch, like it happened long ago.

I turned away. It was easier not to see.

On Thursday Mom stopped me in the hallway. "Don't you think you ought to go to Mr. Vogelman's house and offer your condolences?"

No, I didn't. I didn't think I ought to do anything. Especially talk. There was no reason to push my words out anymore.

I asked, "To who?"

"To *whom,*" Mom said.

"Yeah, OK, to whom?"

"To Frouke," Mom said. "And I think his family has arrived from Chicago."

My attention snapped to the surface. I thought of the girl with braids, Birdman's little bird. I didn't think I wanted to see her—or any of them. It felt like they were swooping in to take him away from me.

So I put it off.

On Friday Mom said, "Sometimes we have to come out of our own grief in order to recognize someone else's."

I hitched up my backpack and brushed past her. My words had burrowed back inside and were stuck there. What good were words anyway?

After school, I picked up my new glasses. Everything zoomed into focus. Walking home, I saw individual blades of grass. I saw moss on roofs. I read words on far-away signs. Now there was no excuse not to see.

The funeral would have been easier if my vision had stayed blurry. Then I wouldn't have had to see how packed the church was or the Channel Six News crew waiting outside. I hadn't realized Birdman was famous. It made me feel small and made Birdman seem unreachable.

Without glasses, I might not have seen Orion and

his family in the back. Or exchanged a long, sorrowful look with Frouke across the pews. Or seen Birdman's family—the dad, the mom, the three kids—just like the portrait in his living room. They had swooped in from across the country and sat in the front pew, and I couldn't help thinking that they should have loved him more—as much as Frouke and I did.

But I did have my glasses, and I did see it all. Maybe that's why I couldn't listen—not to the priest and not to the eulogy Birdman's son gave. I tuned it out.

I thought instead of Rembrandt and his dab of light. Birdman had left behind dabs of light in all his artwork, especially his collaged faces. I wondered if his family could even see it, the new life he gave to old things. I watched them—the younger kids fidgeting, the oldest girl staring vacantly at the stained-glass window. I doubted it.

Elise came over later that day, and Jordyn let us have the bedroom to ourselves. I didn't think I could talk, but when Elise asked, "How was the funeral?" out came a trickle of words that turned to a stream, then a rushing river.

"There were so many flowers and people and news

cameras," I said. "It made me feel like he belonged to them, not me. Like I was just a blip in his life."

"I know it feels that way," she said, "but it's not true."

"How do you know it's not true? You never met him."

"You're right." Elise nodded thoughtfully. "I don't know for sure."

This was not making me feel better.

"But I bet you do," she added.

I thought of my snow angel. I thought of bringing the hope. Maybe I was more than just a blip. Or maybe that's all I was, but at least I'd made him laugh sometimes.

Elise and I were quiet for a while.

"I tried to apologize to Orion," I finally said. "But he wouldn't see me. Do you think he hates me?"

Elise threw my pitiful look right back at me. She had been sympathetic about Birdman. Orion was another story.

"Do *you* think he hates you?"

"I guess not." Orion didn't hate anything. He was calm and reasonable and forgiving. "But I don't think I can face him."

Elise nodded. "Yeah, it's hard. But sometimes the important thing is to show up. And to stay, even when you want to run away."

There was a brittleness to her voice that told me

she spoke from experience. Her father hadn't shown up, hadn't stayed.

I drew in a deep breath. I wanted to be a person who stayed.

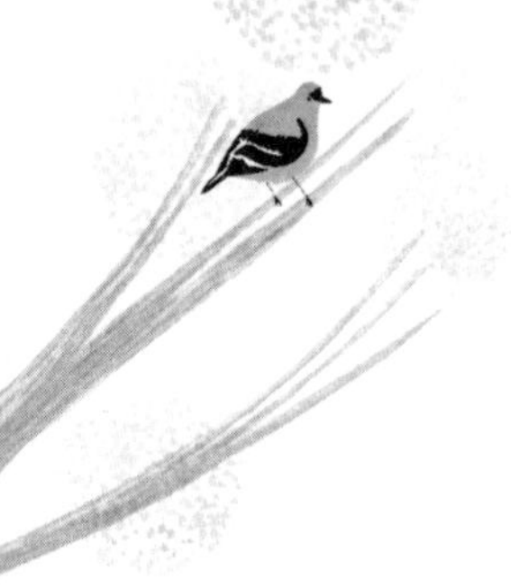

Chapter 39

I paused at the head of Birdman's driveway and placed my hand on the stone pedestal. *I could perch up there and pose as the new glass ball,* I thought. I'd be just as empty. Still, I had to offer my condolences.

Crunching up Birdman's driveway, I remembered that first time—Orion hiding in the rhododendron, me struggling under the weight of the glass ball. Back then, I'd thought I was being brave. Now I came up the driveway full of wobbly hope—hope that if I saw the atelier one last time, I'd feel close to Birdman again. Then I could release the words stuck inside—all the ones I hadn't gotten a chance to say. I could make him mine again.

But even though Birdman was gone, one thing hadn't changed. As always, Frouke blocked the doorway. The pouches under her eyes were swollen. She held a handkerchief beneath her nose to catch the drips. When she saw me, all her hard places went soft.

"*Ja?*"

The first words that leapt to my mind were *knock-knock*. But I couldn't say that, so I said something I'd heard in a movie: "I offer my most sincere condolences."

Frouke blinked, then sniffed. All the soft places stiffened back up. "I *tank* you for your kind regards."

It sounded like an accusation. Behind Frouke, I heard voices. She was about to close the door, but I needed to get inside.

"Wait," I said. "I left something in the atelier."

Luckily, Frouke didn't probe further. She turned without a word and led me down the hallway. With each step, a picture of Birdman became clearer and clearer in my mind, as if I might open the atelier door and find him working there.

As we passed through the living room, a man's voice called from the back of the house. "Frouke, who is it?"

I shrank against the wall. Birdman's son. I couldn't bear to see his family—their faces free from grief and questioning what right I had to be there.

Frouke asked, "You come and meet them?"

I didn't move.

"It is hard, *ja*, but you do it."

I shook my head.

She waved me away in disgust. "You know the way," she said, then, down the hallway, she called, "It is no one."

I felt a twinge of shame but brushed it off. I slipped into the atelier alone. Of course, Birdman wasn't there, but the smell of split wood and lingering paint fumes met me immediately. I opened a drawer and smelled rust. Another drawer smelled of clean metal. They were the smells of broken things and of new life.

After a few minutes, my nose became accustomed, and I no longer smelled Birdman in the atelier. It made me so sad to think I might forget that smell. That I might forget the sound of his hammer striking wood. That I might forget the weight of his droopy eye. That someday I might forget him.

Something on the corner shelf caught my eye—a spray of wire, a collection of knobs, the back of a board. I pulled down the almost-finished portrait of Frouke, and with my fingertips, I stroked the side of the face. Here, I felt Birdman—in the work.

I knew then what I had to do. I would finish it. I would finish it for Birdman. For myself. And even for Frouke.

I pulled down the parts yet to be attached and laid them out on the workbench. At first, I touched the pieces lightly, afraid of ruining the portrait. But soon I was lost in the work. I glued and sanded, smudged and painted. I twisted objects to fit my vision—our vision.

In my head, I heard Birdman's words: *We must not forget the compassion.*

And so, as a finishing touch, I painted the softness I had seen in Frouke for a moment at the door. With tender strokes, I brushed a pinkish skin-color over the cheeks, the chin, the brow.

When I heard a faint creak from the door, I whirled around, expecting for one joyous moment to see Birdman coming toward me. Instead it was Frouke. She thundered down on me. I shielded the portrait with my body.

"Aha! Now comes the monkey out of the sleeve! You come to steal *tings*." She lunged to the right to see around me, but I blocked her.

"No!" I blubbered. "I was only finishing it."

"*You* finish *his* work?" She lunged to the left, but again I was too quick.

"We were working on it together. It was the last thing—" My voice caught in my throat. "I wanted to finish it. For him."

Frouke stilled, but she did not soften. "I will see it."

In her eyes, I saw the hurt. She missed Birdman as much as I did.

I knew she would see the portrait eventually, so I

stepped aside, feeling miserable. Now she would hate me even more.

Frouke's gaze fell to the portrait, and I feared we had made a terrible mistake. Birdman and I had highlighted her most unattractive features: the wart, the square chin, the wiry hair. It must seem to her that Birdman, on the doorstep of death, had been making fun of her. I should have stolen the portrait so that she would never see it.

"Too big," she said, softly.

"What?"

"My wart. It is not so big." Gently, she touched the wart on the side of her nose.

A look came over her face—one I'd never seen before. Her mouth contorted, and her eyes scrunched up like she had to pass some really bad gas.

Oh, no, I realized. *She's going to cry.*

I squeezed my eyes shut. A high, scratchy noise came out of Frouke, a long ribbon of sound. I opened my eyes and saw the corners of her mouth turned up. She was smiling. More than that—the strange ribbon of sound was laughter.

I could hardly believe it. Frouke was laughing.

The shock must have been painted brightly on my face, because when she caught her breath, Frouke said,

"You *tink* I can't laugh at myself? I know what I am." She ran a stubby thumb over the forehead of the portrait. "*Everyting* else he got just right."

I didn't mention that I had done much of it. I still couldn't believe she liked it. We hadn't forgotten the compassion after all.

Then it dawned on me—I had finally made Frouke laugh! Not with any joke, but simply by holding up a mirror.

A laugh erupted out of me. Frouke began laughing again too, and before long fat tears rolled down our cheeks. We doubled over with laughter.

I wasn't sure how long we laughed, but finally, sighing and wiping her eyes, Frouke again touched the portrait. "This was the last thing he did?"

"I think so," I said.

Then she started to cry. So did I. Our joy and sorrow mixed together into a big swish of color, and neither of us could tell the difference. Neither of us cared. Frouke pulled me to her bosom and held onto me like I was the last thing she had.

We saw each other. Finally.

Before I left, Frouke asked me to wait. She hurried out

of the atelier. Rubens looked down from his poster with a frank smile. I re-read the quote:

"My talent is such that no undertaking, however vast in size . . . has ever surpassed my courage."—Peter Paul Rubens

I smiled up at him. Many undertakings still surpassed my courage, but now, at least, I felt ready to show up.

Frouke returned carrying my secret sketchbook, the one with my hopeless drawing, the one I'd left the day Birdman had blacked out his painting. I had nearly forgotten about it.

"He took your draw book with him to hospital," she said.

"Really?" My breath caught in my throat. Tears leapt to my eyes again. Had he taken it with him to look at my drawings? All this time I had feared Birdman forgot me each time he was away.

"He didn't want you to see him like that. Too proud."

I wished Frouke had told me he was in the hospital, but I couldn't be angry with her after what we'd just shared. I wished I could have seen Birdman one last time, knowing it would be the last. I would have made sure he knew that I would always bring the hope. I would have let him know how grateful I was for all he'd taught me. And I would have told him that I finally understood that seeing my tree was just like doing every hard thing. I'd never be done.

My vision blurred with tears. Frouke was a dark figure against the white light of the huge windows. I squinted to feather the light, and everywhere there were wings, all around us, brushing against us, nudging us toward each other.

Birdman would have liked that.

I laughed aloud.

"Another joke?" Frouke asked.

I shook my head. It seemed right to tell her. "Wings," I said, waving at the light. "Wings are everywhere!"

She blinked around at the room. She squinted. Then she smiled. "*Ja,* they are."

Chapter 40

As soon as I emerged from Birdman's driveway, I saw Orion standing in the street between our two houses. Something about him was different, but I couldn't pinpoint it from this distance.

I began walking toward him. He had come to me, but I would have to come the rest of the way. It didn't feel like such a hard thing.

I passed the bird tree, twittering again with finches. I passed crocuses poking their heads out in Mrs. Davenport's yard.

When I was close enough to see Orion's face, and the hurt still written there, I felt a pang of sorrow for the time we had missed while I wasn't paying attention. We could have shared so much. Now all I had to share was grief.

Finally I reached him, and we stood before each other, silent.

I thought of the Dutch word Birdman had taught me—*zwijgen*—and how in English it meant we *are* silent, but in Dutch we had to actively *do* it. At the time, I hadn't grasped the distinction. Now I did.

Orion and I stood before each other and *zwijged*—or however you say it for two people. Together we built a silence, fragile and fleeting, like a sand castle. We patted everything we knew and felt into it.

Orion lifted one shoulder and dropped it back down—a gesture that said, *I see you, Clarity. I see you, and I understand.*

It was like a clean ocean breeze washing over me.

I could have left it there. But sometimes gestures aren't enough. Sometimes the words must be said.

"Orion, I'm sorry for the way I treated you . . . and for shoving you and yelling at you."

I expected his forgiveness to be instant, for him to say, *It's OK* or *No worries,* but instead he held my gaze for a long time. Finally he said, "That was not OK."

"I know. I'm sorry." I wanted to be past this moment, but I knew we had to go through it to come out the other side.

"You know what was even worse?" he said. "What I still don't get? Why didn't you tell me about Mr. Vogelman?"

I looked down. He was right to be hurt. "I don't know.

It was stupid of me. I should have told you from the very beginning."

"I felt like you didn't trust me. Like you were leaving me behind."

I winced at how thoughtless I'd been. "Can you forgive me?"

Orion looked at me steadily, then a sly grin spread on his face. "I'll give it a try."

I grinned too, filled with relief—we were halfway there already.

"I'm sorry about Mr. Vogelman," he said. "I know he meant a lot to you."

Suddenly I realized what was different about Orion. There was a bright spot in his eye, like Rembrandt's dab of light. Like the light from spent stars. A light that hinted at worlds inside him I'd never thought to wonder about.

I knew that what Orion and I shared was real and strong and lasting. But I wanted to go back and recover what we'd missed.

"That painting of our tree," I said, "I'd like to give it back to you . . . if you still want it." Luckily, it had dried without warping.

"Of course I want it."

"We can hang it in the annex again."

Orion shook his head. "We can't, Clara."

"Why not?"

"The annex isn't ours anymore."

"Because of Elise? I don't mind that she was there. I want us to all be friends. I was just . . . jealous." There. I'd said the word.

"No," Orion said, "that's not what I mean. I'm talking about the remodel. Mom and Javier want it cleared out so they can tear down the walls."

I thought of the Christmas lights and the gray days of winter we had spent there with raindrops pinging on the ductwork overhead. But those had been days of me not really seeing Orion. In truth, our annex was already gone.

We walked a circuit of the street like we always used to, then sat on the curb and watched the fleet of finches making great loops in the sky.

"Elise said your presentation went well," he said.

"Yeah," I said with a twinge of pride.

"So, you're going to start giving speeches now?"

I swatted his arm.

And then he asked me.

"What would you have said at Mr. Vogelman's funeral, if you'd been up there in front of all those people? If you could choke out the words, Clara?"

I didn't know the answer to that, so I swatted his arm again. "Birdman," I whispered.

"Huh?"

"He's Birdman to me."

And then I told Orion everything. I explained about Birdman's name and how he called me "little potato." I talked about him teaching me to look for the essence. About how he found new lives for old things.

"You would have liked that," I said. "You would have liked him."

We *zwijged* some more, and the birds swooped close on the way back to their tree—a flowering plum getting ready to bloom.

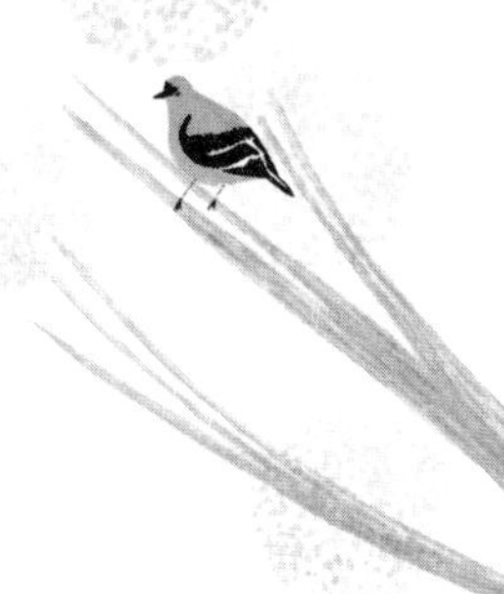

Chapter 41

January turned to February, revealing more glimpses of spring. Orion's question revolved like a Ferris wheel in my head. Each time it swung to the top, I thought I might brush the sky.

But I didn't have an answer.

Though I had found a way to unplug my words for Frouke and Orion and Elise, I still carried unsaid words for Birdman. Maybe grief was like that. Mom said it took time. Maybe you just had to learn to live with it.

Orion and I cleaned out the annex. We took down the Christmas lights, dragged the beanbags upstairs, and untacked my art postcards from the walls. I gathered up Mr. Ya-yo and my art supplies. They didn't feel sacred anymore.

"Remember when we said we were going to hide here?" I asked.

"Yeah." Orion laughed.

"I was going to hide from every hard thing. Seems silly now, doesn't it?"

"Childish." Orion picked up his box of knots and balanced the small table on top. "I guess that's it."

The space was empty now, lit only by secondhand daylight coming through the open door. We left our secret annex for the last time. In the coming weeks, its walls would be torn down, and it would become part of the house.

I gave it one last glance but didn't feel sad. We'd outgrown it.

February lifted, and March sprung up. Daffodils began to yellow. Grape hyacinth poked up their purple heads. Forsythia waved their budding wands. A new spark filled the air, and it seemed to shimmer between my house and Orion's.

But whenever I looked down the street to the empty pedestal, something stuck in my throat, and I had to swallow it down.

It was then that the painting arrived on our doorstep.

The doorbell rang while Mom was changing a poopy diaper. She called down the hallway, "Girls! Will one of you get that?"

"Not it," Jordyn said without looking up from her phone.

"I'll get it," I said, as if it was exactly what I wanted to do.

I opened the door, but no one was there. I looked down. Leaning against the railing was a rectangular, flattish package wrapped in brown paper. No stamps. No address. But scrawled across the front in strange wobbly letters were the words, *For the little potato.*

I stared at the package, not moving.

Mom came up behind me. "Is it for you?"

"I don't know." Of course it was for me—that much was obvious—but I was suddenly so full of hope and fear that I couldn't say anything definite.

Benny tried to push through my legs, squealing when I held them firm.

"There's a note," Mom said, pulling a folded piece of flowery stationery from the side of the package. She tried to pass it to me, but I clasped my hands together.

"You read it."

She unfolded the paper, and I held my breath.

"It says, 'He intended this for you. Frouke.'"

I picked up the package. It was heavy, and it clanged as I moved it. I tore a bit of the brown paper away, then stopped. I gazed down the street to the finches in the bird tree.

"What are you waiting for?" Mom asked. "Open it."

I didn't know what I was waiting for. I couldn't put my hope into words. I'd been longing for another moment with Birdman, some message from him, some last word. I'd never thought it would actually happen, but here it was, at my feet.

I took a breath and, in one clean motion, ripped the paper from the package.

Behind me, Mom gasped, but my breath was caught in my lungs. I was so full. I never wanted to exhale again.

Looking straight at me was a portrait of myself, fashioned from objects in Birdman's drawers. The hair was made from feathers so light that they fell forward and back as if swayed by secret breezes. For my eyes, he had used the old-fashioned bicycle bells we had such fun ringing. The shape and size were the same as my glasses, with the thumb pads positioned at the top corners to resemble eyelashes.

"Amazing," Mom marveled. "It looks just like you."

I saw something else in the portrait, something more than what I knew of myself. There was strength in the jaw.

Determination in the brow. Wide-openness in the eyes. He had seen my faults. He had seen my strengths. He had not forgotten the compassion.

Tears brimmed over. Mom held the portrait while I wiped my eyes.

Birdman had seen me—really seen me.

Benny finally broke through my legs and came around to pat my thighs.

"Ah-tee!" he called. "Ah-tee!"

I knelt with the portrait. Benny went straight for the eyes, banging with the flat of his hand, producing a dull *ting*.

"Listen," I said, pressing down on the thumb pad.

Driiiiing! The bell erupted in a shrill ring. Benny's face lit up in delight. His little fingers didn't have enough force to ring the bells himself, so I rang them over and over again.

The joyous sound rose and took flight. I remembered ringing the bells with Birdman and the lightness we both felt. Now, with Benny, the heaviness lifted from my shoulders, as if I might rise on wings of my own. When the last ring died away, Mom said, "Should we hang this in the living room?"

"Sure," I said, feeling like there was room for me in this family after all.

Chapter 42

With the portrait hung in the living room and the secret annex cleared out, the time had come for me to start drawing again. I dug my secret sketchbook out from under my bed. I hadn't opened it since Frouke gave it back to me.

I opened to one of my old drawings. It looked like a jumble of dark swoops across the page, but I remembered my exact feelings while drawing it. It had been summer, and I had been frustrated that Benny got all the attention. How childish that seemed now.

Suddenly I noticed the tiny black words scrawled at the bottom. *The Storm,* it said.

My breath stopped. I knew that handwriting.

I turned to the next page, a drawing of the creek forcing its way through the trees. Only it didn't look like water or trees. I had been drawing with my glasses off.

At the bottom, in the same handwriting, were the words: *I think of water. It smooths everything in its path.*

I flipped through the pages more frantically. Each one had a comment—sometimes a word, sometimes whole sentences. With each page, the handwriting grew more spidery.

I imagined Birdman lying in a hospital bed, pen in hand, turning the pages of my sketchbook. Seeing my drawings. Seeing me.

I turned another page and there was my hopeless drawing. At the bottom, Birdman had written, *Where is the hope?* The last word seemed to fade off the page, so faint was the pressure of the pen.

For a long time, I stared at those words, thinking of Birdman, lying in the hospital with only that drawing as his last message from me. It was so wrong. If I could go back in time and do one thing differently, I would take that sketchbook with me when I left Birdman's atelier. Maybe I couldn't have changed his cancer or his family problems or even him blacking out his own painting, but I could have taken my hopeless drawing with me.

I squeezed my eyes shut, but still the tears slid out. Finally I turned the page, and there was another drawing, one I'd forgotten. It was the bird tree. I was always trying to capture that moment when every bird rose from the tree at the same instant.

At the bottom, Birdman had written: *Hope.*

I turned the page. Blank. Another page. Blank also. From there on, everything was blank. No final message. Just page after page of white space with that last fluttering word—*Hope*—echoing through.

I pressed the sketchbook to my chest and smiled to think that *Hope* might have been Birdman's last thought before dying. Now I knew what I had given him. And now I recognized the word stuck inside. It was ready for release.

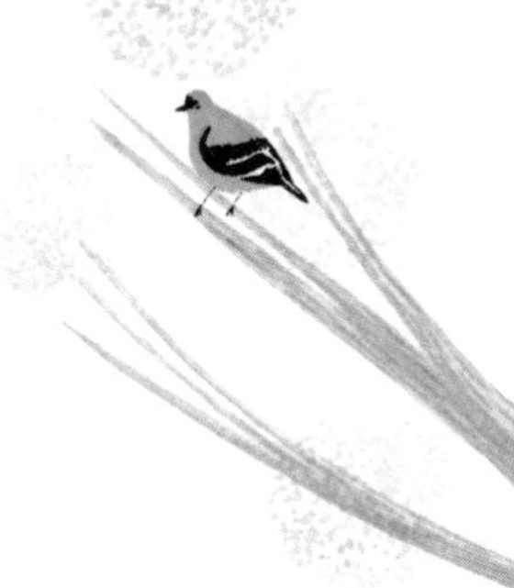

Chapter 43

It was a crisp March day. Orion was tying a knot for me to untangle as we strolled down Rock Street. The flowering plums had bloomed early, sending tiny pinkish petals spiraling down like snow.

Orion handed me the knot, a big, ugly mess.

"Ugh," I said. "You won't go easy on me, will you?"

"Never," he said.

Behind us, the finches chattered in their tree. I worked on the knot as we came to the dead end. Birdman had left Frouke his house. She'd sell it eventually, but for now she was busy organizing his affairs. Sometimes I visited to help catalogue his paintings—and to exchange jokes. In the fall, there would be a retrospective show in Portland—a look back at Birdman's life's work. Aunt Lindy had promised to take me.

Orion and I circled the empty pedestal, and I wondered

what had become of the glass ball. If I saw it now, I wouldn't be afraid to look into the crack.

I had the knot almost untangled when we came to the bird tree. Suddenly all the birds fell silent and rose into the air. Usually, they rose, did a couple of loops in the sky as one body, then settled back into their tree. But this time, they kept rising, kept flying upward and outward as if each one was heading for its own star past all that blue.

Orion and I watched until, one by one, the finches disappeared into the sky. Maybe there were clouds. Maybe the sun was too bright. But we couldn't see them anymore.

A note sounded inside me. It was high and free and almost painful. Time to let out the word I'd been keeping inside.

"Goodbye," I whispered.

"What?" Orion asked.

It was then that I knew. I knew what I would have said about Birdman, what I would say to anyone who asked. I would tell about the wings—his and mine and everybody's.

I looked into Orion's eyes and knew that all the seeing in the world couldn't make something different from what it was. Death was death. Holding on wouldn't change that fact. But maybe, just maybe, if I let it go, let it fly away, maybe something good and beautiful would fly back to me next year.

I reached out and took Orion's hand in mine. Our fingers laced together, and it felt tingly-strange, like the start of something good. Orion had that dopey smile again.

"C'mon," I said, leading him up the street. "I have some things to share with you."

As we walked, I could feel each place where our skin touched. Part of me wanted to separate our fingers, but Orion held my hand firmly. This was a knot I wouldn't untangle.

Acknowledgments

A flock of people helped me craft this story, and I am grateful to each of them. To my early readers:

My critique group, the Slushbusters—Joan, Stephanie, Sarah, Michelle, Bridget, Alison—who kept meeting with me even when I moved across an ocean or a continent. Their feedback made the story better and better.

The Community Roots girls, who helped keep my eleven-year-old believable.

Dawn Tacker, Cory Freeman, and Sarah Dalisky, who read the story when I thought I was finished and gave enough glowing feedback for me to tackle the tougher comments (and another revision).

To the experts:

Shay Copple, speech-language pathologist, who answered my many questions about Clara's speech difficulties. Any mistakes are my own.

My agent, Shannon Hassan, who has had to keep believing in this story (and me) for a long time. I thank her for her diligence.

My editor, Alison Deering, whose keen eye and insightful questions kept pushing me when I so wanted to be done. She let me talk it out when I needed to and then let me figure it out on my own.

The entire Capstone team who cheered this book on and worked to make it shine, especially Michelle Bisson, who pointed out things I'd tried to dance around, and copy editor Sara Biren, who caught some glaring errors.

Rosanna Tasker for the gorgeous cover art and the other amazing art she puts into the world.

To my support and inspiration:

The Society of Children's Book Writers and Illustrators—what an amazing and encouraging community of storytellers!

My art students, who delight in new forms of expression and inspire me to keep doing the hard work of creating.

My inspiration for Birdman's artwork came from my first cousin once removed, Franz Leinfelder, who lives in Germany and creates stunning relief-collages out of objects he finds, sometimes along railroad tracks. Here is his website: www.franz-leinfelder.de.

The large oak tree featured in the book is based on an actual tree living in the Oregon Garden in Silverton. I spent many hours hanging out with this four-hundred-year-old Signature Oak. I didn't draw it as many times as Clara, but I had toddlers to babysit and she didn't.

And most of all, to my dear friends and family, who provided all kinds of support, from chocolate breaks to child care, from "You can do it!" to "Let's get you out of this dark office and have some fun." Extra special thanks to my husband, Michiel Nankman, who helped with Dutch grammar and expressions, Frouke's jokes, and anything else I felt unsure about. He helped so much that I can hardly believe he still hasn't read the book!

To my son, Alexander, for respecting the closed office door. To my sweet daughters, Annabel and Mieke, who listened to me read aloud and gasped and teared up in all the right places, giving me the courage to push through one more revision. Thank you forever!